Metaphorosis

June 2021

Beautifully made speculative fiction

Also from Metaphorosis

Verdage

Reading 5X5 x2: Duets
Score – an SFF symphony
Reading 5X5: Readers' Edition
Reading 5X5: Writers' Edition

Metaphorosis Magazine

Metaphorosis: Best of 20xx
Metaphorosis 20xx: The Complete Stories
annual issues, from 2016

Monthly issues

Vestige

Tower of Mud and Straw
by Yaroslav Barsukov
2021 Nebula Finalist!

Plant Based Press

Best Vegan Science Fiction & Fantasy
annual issues, from 2016

from B. Morris Allen:
Susurrus
Allenthology: Volume I
Tocsin: and other stories
Start with Stones: collected stories
Metaphorosis: a collection of stories

Metaphorosis

June 2021

edited by
B. Morris Allen

ISSN: 2573-136X (online)
ISBN: 978-1-64076-201-5 (e-book)
ISBN: 978-1-64076-202-2 (paperback)

from
Metaphorosis Publishing

Neskowin

June 2021

The Secret Keeper

Pauline Yates

Keeping a secret is dangerous. Secrets mess with emotions and can cause illness from depression, anxiety, and stress. The darker the secret, the heavier the burden; it can shorten your life by years. Even Demigods, like Mother and me, need to be cautious when keeping a secret. We're gifted with powers to balance emotions, but if we reveal a secret, we'll suffer its burden. It's crucial we stay strong, because we help battle the gods who draw their power from misery and suffering.

Like Hades. He doesn't mind if a person troubled by a secret dies young. He draws his power from the souls of the dead. And in his realm, the bearer suffers their burden three times worse. But we have Harpocrates, the god of silence, on our side. He uses hope to encourage a bearer to reveal their secret and clear their conscience. To deliver hope, he needs a Secret Keeper, and now I'm sixteen, that's what I'm about to become.

"Repeat after me," Mother says. "Listen without—"

"—judgment and heal the harm," I say, not needing her help. I've committed these vows to heart. "Bind the secret with a Keeper's charm. If by fault I break the faith, suffer the burden the thorns keep safe."

Mother slips a charming binding ring onto my finger. The gold band, engraved with a pattern of linked roses, is the token of a Secret Keeper.

"How much hope do you give?" she asks.

"Only enough to ease their pain; too much hope is a secret's gain." Giving too much hope can make the bearer believe that keeping their secret won't cause them harm.

"And how much burden do you take?" Mother says, her voice low like a brewing storm.

I sigh, wishing Mother weren't so melodramatic. I know what to do. But she expects an answer. "Only enough that hope shines through. Though it harms, they need the burden, too." Removing all the burden takes away the incentive to reveal the secret. That defeats our purpose.

Mother smiles. "Balancing emotions is tricky, but your charm will help."

I raise my hand to the rising sun and admire the ring. The charm curls from the band and weaves around my fingers like a glittering ribbon of light. Feeling its power makes me giddy with excitement.

Now I can heal using a true god's power. Until now, I've only ever had demigod powers to work with. That power allows me to grow herbs from nothing to make the remedies we sell to the local townsfolk. We're the talk around town because of their potency, but we hide our true identity. Mother 'has a green thumb'. I'm 'the homeschooled girl'. Receiving the charm makes me feel like I've graduated.

Lowering my hand, I touch the charm with my finger. It shapes into a glittering rose, Harpocrates' symbol. He created the charm, but I fuel its strength by imagining where I find hope. All Secret Keepers have their preference. For me, hope is in a sunrise, in a rainbow, in seedlings bursting through the soil. Hope is also in my desire to be the best Keeper Harpocrates has ever had.

"The ability to heal the harm caused by a secret is a rare and wondrous gift," Mother says. "However, Harpocrates does not give this charm freely. You are now his servant, as I am, and my mother before me. Harpocrates uses his power to keep hope alive in the world and expects you to do the same. Without hope, the world would fall under the influence of those gods who favor darkness and despair."

She opens her hand, revealing her ring. Years of use make it appear fluid, like a circle of lava. Her charm curls from the band and takes the shape of a burnished gold rose, similar to mine. Mother blows on it. The rose dissolves into a spray of mist that fills the air with a mixture of sweet and pungent perfume.

Turning her hand, the bitter perfume overpowers the sweet. "Polemos draws his power from conflict," she says. "Oizys, misery. Dolos, pain." She tilts her hand again and the sweet perfume overpowers the bitter. "Hestia, compassion, Eros, love, and of course, Harpocrates, hope. There cannot be light without dark, but, tipped out of balance, chaos will ensue." With a flick of her hand, the scents collide. They splatter on the ground like splashes of water.

"Do you think we make a difference?" I ask, tilting my hand so my charm dances on my finger. "We're only demigods. What good is our strength in a battle for power between the gods?"

"You're stronger than you think. The strength of all Secret Keepers runs in your blood. Collectively, we are Harpocrates' most powerful allies. Just be mindful of your vows and replace the burden you remove with hope. You don't want to leave a person feeling as dark and empty as the day Hades stole Persephone from this world."

"Does a burdened soul give Hades extra power?"

"No, but he benefits by receiving a soul quicker. A burden left unattended leads to premature death," Mother says. "Otherwise, he has no interest in warring for power. It's why he lets Persephone return for half the year. But don't dismiss him. Now that you channel Harpocrates' power, Hades will watch to see if you stay true to your vows. He's never broken an oath, and values the laws of morality over everything."

It's a value I share. Secret Keepers heal, they don't harm. Breaking my vow would also desecrate the moral law of our kind.

I glance across the gardens at the many roses that grow between the herbs. All were grown by Mother to keep the secrets she heard. Each sprouts thorns glistening with the secret's burden—guilt, sorrow, remorse. In all our history, no Secret Keeper has ever broken her vows. Suffering any of those emotions would be a deserved punishment. Revealing a secret breaks trust. Breaking trust would destroy hope, and we're tasked with keeping hope alive.

But I needn't worry. Even without history on my side, I'll enjoy showing Hades how committed to my vows I can be.

With the commitment ceremony complete, I revert to my daily chores. Weeding the garden. Growing more herbs to replace those we've used. We're out of dried lavender, so I fetch my gardening clippers. As I snip the stems, my charm grows brighter. It draws hope from my thoughts about lavender's healing qualities.

Customers arrive throughout the day. Some seek a herbal remedy. Others request a pot of living herbs to grow in their gardens. All wander through the gardens while Mother prepares their purchase. All ask the same question on their return.

"Are the roses for sale?"

I've lost count of the number of times I say no because of Mother's fondness for the flowers. I smooth over their disappointment by revealing it's why I share the flower's name. I don't mind the interruptions. Before I became a Secret Keeper, I'd try to guess if a customer had a secret, to no avail. Now that I have Harpocrates' charm, it changes everything.

"Should we hear all secrets?" I ask, after selling a girl my age a jar of comfrey for her mother's arthritis. I'm worried I missed the chance to hear my first secret. The charm grew warm in my hand and my mind filled with an image of the girl kissing a boy.

"Only if you want to," Mother says as she ties a string around the lavender stems to hang them in the kitchen. "Happy secrets can still cause worry, spoiling a surprise, for example. But those secrets get revealed in due course, so we rarely bother. It's the dark secrets that need our help the most." She glances out the front door. "Your chance to learn the difference has arrived."

A woman in her early twenties approaches the house. Her face is pale and the dark circles beneath her eyes suggest something is amiss. My charm curls into my hand, but no images suggesting a secret fill my mind.

"How do you know she has a dark secret?" I ask, wondering how Mother can detect what I can't.

"A lifetime of practice," she says. "Now, always try to coax out their secret first. Offering them someone to confide in works as well as the charm."

"Yes, Mother."

"If they won't tell, which many don't, use the charm. But remember, dark secrets are not pleasant."

"Yes, Mother."

I hurry from the house. Her warning fills my stomach with fluttering butterflies. Mustering my bravest smile, I approach the woman. "Hello. I'm Rose. Can I help you?"

"Hi. I'm Miranda. But everyone calls me Mim." She fidgets with the cuff of her sleeve and looks toward the gardens. "Your roses are beautiful. I admired them from the road." She hesitates, then turns her attention to the herbs. "Would you have a herbal remedy to help with forgetfulness? It's for my mother," she adds. "She has Alzheimer's."

"I'm sorry to hear that. How bad is she?"

Mim sighs. "Stage seven. She's in a nursing home and not expected to live much longer. We're trying to keep her comfortable."

"That must be difficult." I motion her to a table and chairs set up on the porch.

"I have to remind my mother who I am every day," Mim admits, walking with me to the porch. "It's hard."

The butterflies in my stomach close their wings and settle. It appears Mim is just exhausted from caring for a dying parent.

"Gingko will help your mother," I say, pulling out a chair and encouraging Mim to sit. "It's wonderful for helping with memory problems. And chamomile for you, to help you cope. Would you like to try some chamomile tea while I prepare a remedy for your mother?"

"That would be lovely," Mim says, sinking into the chair.

I hurry inside to boil the kettle, but Mother stands with a steaming pot of tea, already made.

"An infusion of chamomile," she whispers, handing me the pot. "I couldn't help overhearing. I'll prepare the gingko. You heal Mim."

"She doesn't have a secret," I whisper. "She's exhausted from caring for her mother."

Mother raises an eyebrow. "Are you sure? What does your charm tell you?"

I glance at my ring. The charm dances along the band, making the ring glow like fire. Frowning at my ineptitude, I grab a cup from the kitchen bench and return to Mim.

"Mother will prepare the gingko, but what about you?" I ask, pouring the tea and sitting in the chair opposite her. "You said 'we', before. Do you have other family members that can help?"

"Only my brother," Mim says, taking the cup of chamomile. "He's not around at the moment. He works away." She gulps her tea, her face turning bright red.

I don't need the charm to know she is lying. I wonder if Mim's secret involves her brother. Though itching to use my charm, I follow Mother's advice and offer Mim someone she can confide in.

Looking toward the roses, I sigh. "I love our roses, too. Do you know the story about Aphrodite's son? He gave Harpocrates a rose in return for keeping his mother's indiscretions secret." I pause. "I learned that in my Greek Mythology lessons."

"I didn't know that," Mim says, lowering her cup.

"It's only a myth, of course. But Aphrodite's son was lucky he found a confidant in Harpocrates. Imagine going through life having to keep something to yourself. It would place so much burden on your conscience."

Mim's cheeks flush redder. "It would be horrible, I suppose."

"Worse than horrible. If you don't clear your conscience in life, you'll suffer the burden three times worse in death."

"You do?" Mim asks, shifting uncomfortably.

"Yes." I sigh again, then clasp my hands and rest them on the table. "But a conscience is easy to clear. Confiding in another person will lift the burden." I pause because Mim looks mortified. "I suppose revealing a secret can be difficult."

"Impossibly difficult," Mim mutters, clenching her hands around her cup.

I reach across the table and place my hand over hers. "If you need to, you can confide in me. I'm a healer, which is the same as a doctor, so anything you say is confidential."

Mim's mouth parts as though she's about to accept my offer and spill her secret. But then she shakes her head. "Nothing's wrong," she says. "I appreciate the help, but I'm just worried about my mother."

"Of course you are," I say. "Keep in mind what I said, though. There's more truth in myth than we realize."

I'm not disappointed I couldn't coax out her secret. That's why Harpocrates gave us the charm. Mim keeps her secret buried for a reason. But she's so overwhelmed by dark emotions, she can't see the damage keeping a secret does to her. What she needs now is hope, to help her see that she doesn't have to suffer alone and in silence.

"It must be difficult caring for your mother on your own," I say, squeezing her hand. As though sensing it's time to go to work, the charm jumps from the ring. It shapes into a ribbon of light and winds around our hands, binding us together as one. Mim can't see the charm; it's invisible to her. But it exudes hope's calm confidence, and the subtle effect helps Mim relax.

"It's hard," Mim says, squeezing my hand in return. "I show her photos to help jog her memory. Sometimes they work. I also play her favorite music..."

While Mim talks about her mother, the charm fades through her skin to go in search of her secret. In what feels like an eyeblink, an image filters into my mind; Mim and a man who could be her twin. The charm has found the secret, but as Mother warned, it's not pleasant—

Mim's brother died two weeks ago, but Mim keeps his death secret. Her mother asks about him every day, and every day Mim says he'll see her tomorrow. Mim thinks it would be better if her mother died hoping to see her son than grieving his death. She hasn't even told the nursing

19

home staff. She doesn't want anyone telling her mother the truth. But pretending her brother is still alive prevents her from mourning. And guilt about the lie to her mother tears her apart.

It takes all my strength not to react to the secret and keep listening to Mim talk about her mother. I wasn't prepared to hear a secret so sad. Squeezing back tears, I trust the charm to know how much burden to remove and how much hope to give. In my distressed state, I'd mess it up.

The charm skims across Mim's conscience. It removes a layer of grief and guilt then replaces them with the hope I conjured when picking the lavender. It gives just enough hope to balance Mim's emotions, and already Mim's tense grip on my hand relaxes. Then the charm carries the burden it removed to me, and curls back into the ring.

It didn't look like a lot, but the grief and guilt hit my heart with a heavy thud. Easing my hand from Mim's, I clasp my hands, drawing comfort from the warmth in the ring. Mim stops talking and heaves a sigh. Then she picks up her cup and finishes her tea.

"This is lovely," she says. "What did you say it was?"

"Chamomile," I say, forcing a smile.

I'm pleased with her lightened mood. Hope shines in her eyes and her troubled expression fades. She doesn't know that I heard her secret, or that the charm removed some of her burdens. But the hope she received should help her consider whether it's worth keeping her secret. What she decides to do is up to her, but at least now she's not blind to her choices.

The layer of dark emotions throbs through my veins. Needing to trap it in thorns, I stand to fetch the gingko so I can send Mim on her way. Mother steps onto the porch holding two paper packets.

"Chamomile tea for you, and gingko for your mother," she says, handing Mim the packets. "The instructions are in the bags. I'm sorry to hear about your mother. The gingko will help make her last days more pleasurable. Be sure to look after yourself, too."

"I will," Mim says, standing and taking the packets. "Thank you, Rose. The tea has made me feel better already." She hesitates. "I liked your story about the roses. It's given me a lot to think about."

Then she hurries from the porch, clutching the packets to her chest.

I'm relieved the hope is working, but I'm more grateful for her swift departure. Clutching at the ache in my heart, I hurry to the garden.

Finding space in a garden where none of Mother's roses grow, I crouch and sow Mim's secret into the soil. The ground around my fingers glows the same golden color as the charm. The emotions I took from Mim leach out, leaving me dizzy with relief. Pulling my hands from the soil, I roll back onto my heels and watch the secret grow.

A stem pushes through the soil. Tall and slender, it sprouts long thorns, green with guilt. Grief glistens like dewdrops on the tips. Standing, I cup my hands around the rose that blooms at the top. Red petals release a heavy scent that makes me think of funerals and death.

Stepping back, I study the rose. I'm elated that my first time hearing a secret proceeded exactly as expected, but I'm also uneasy.

Mim's secret was not pleasant, and I may hear darker secrets than hers. Though I trapped Mim's emotions in thorns, I underestimated the impact those emotions had on me. I hope I haven't also underestimated the strength needed to stay true to my vows.

Later in the day, I kneel beside Mother and help harvest evening primrose before the light fades. I drop more seed pods than I collect because I'm distracted by an image of Hades laughing at me for thinking it's easy to keep a secret.

"Mother? Have you ever heard a secret that is so bad, you don't have the strength to keep it?"

"Find the strength," Mother says. "Otherwise you'll destroy the hope you gave and suffer the secret's burden."

I glance around the garden. In the dying light, the thorns on Mim's rose appear to weep. But a rose growing behind hers draws my attention. It's grown in that spot longer than I've been alive. The red petals reek with an intoxicating perfume. The stem is thick and covered in large mottled-red thorns that speak of something nasty. I shudder to think what burden they trap and wonder where Mother finds the strength to keep the secret.

I'm about to ask when the rose wilts and the petals turn gray.

"Mother," I gasp, my heart leaping into my throat. "That rose died."

Mother stands and walks over to the rose. "Hope shines a light on choice, but sometimes that's still not enough to stop a secret going to the grave."

Scrambling to my feet, I follow. I've seen roses die before, but it hits harder now that I'm a Secret Keeper. Death doesn't release us from our vows. We're still bound to keep the secret. And we can still suffer the burden.

A milky-white mist rises from the ground in front of me. Mother grabs my arm and pulls me away. The mist takes the shape of a translucent figure; the ghost of an old man. My charm must enhance my sight. I've seen ghosts before, too, but never with such clarity. I didn't realize the depth of three-fold suffering.

The man's eyes sink into his skull and his mouth hangs open as though dragged down by weights. He reaches for the rose, but the thorns stab holes in his fingers. His face contorts as though feeling actual pain. Turning to Mother, he stretches his arms toward her.

"I've heard your secret," Mother says. "Hope showed you choices and you made yours. Accept your fate and go. I will not help you in death." She waves the ghost away. The mist disperses, but leaves a chill in the air.

"They're drawn here by the scent of their rose," Mother says. Pulling out the entire rose plant, she tosses it onto the mulch pile. "They forget that the cause of their misery in death is that they didn't clear their conscience in life. But don't let a ghost's suffering tempt you to hear their secret again. Emotions in a soul can't be balanced like in a conscience. If you try to remove some burden, you'll end up taking the lot and have to fill the soul with hope. That would allow the soul to be reborn, and Hades would lose his servant. He would demand the Keeper's soul to compensate, and Harpocrates would oblige. He values our servitude, but would strip your power to conjure hope to avoid a war with Hades.

Mother's words are as chilling as the cold left by the ghost. I thought Harpocrates would protect his servants, since we pledged our loyalty to him. To learn he'd strip my powers in favor of keeping good relations with Hades leaves a sour taste in my mouth. I wonder if we're nothing more than pawns in a power game between the gods.

I fall asleep resenting my commitment to a god who will not protect my allegiance and wake to pouring rain. My resentful thoughts must anger Harpocrates; the rain doesn't ease for three days. If he is showing me what a world without hope looks like, he paints the picture well. I stare in dismay at our wrecked gardens. Then I see the woman.

Fighting the wind to hold an umbrella over her head, she sloshes through the puddles at our front gate. Hurrying outside, I welcome her onto the porch. It's Mrs. Peterson, the elegant yet tight-lipped town mayor's wife. When she steps onto the porch, she sniffs back a sneeze.

Mother appears in the doorway behind me. "Good gracious," she says, taking the umbrella from Mrs. Peterson and shaking it dry. "It's no time to be out in this weather, Mrs. Peterson. Rose, boil the kettle. A pot of tea is in order."

Hurrying inside, I light the burner and set the kettle to boil. Mother and Mrs. Peterson sit at the kitchen table.

"My daughter, Rose," Mother says, introducing me.

"Rose, like the flowers," Mrs. Peterson says, placing her purse on the table and extending her hand. "And just as beautiful."

Blushing at the compliment, I shake her hand. My charm dances around my fingers, alerting me to what I should have guessed from her sniffles. Mrs. Peterson has a secret.

"How is your husband?" Mother asks. "Worn out from running the town, I imagine?"

"His work is his life, and he'll not hear otherwise," Mrs. Peterson says. "But the reason for my intrusion..." Her nose wrinkles, then she sneezes into her hands.

I fetch a box of tissues from the cupboard and slide it across the table. Mrs. Peterson plucks out a tissue and blows her nose. "Thank you, dear," she says. "Such dismal weather. As I was saying, my intrusion—"

"It's no intrusion," Mother says. "Rose? The tea?"

I fetch the kettle and make a pot of herbal tea. When I return to the table, my charm jumps into my hand. It weaves around my fingers as though trying to get my attention. Mrs. Peterson's secret must be bad for my charm to react with such intensity.

"I was driving past and saw your roses," Mrs. Peterson says. "I'd like to buy a bunch. My husband likes a well-presented office. Our usual supplier's flowers are lackluster by comparison."

"The roses aren't for sale," I say, giving my usual response.

Mrs. Peterson purses her lips. "If it's a question of money, my husband will pay well."

I glance at Mother, wondering if she detects the tinge of desperation in Mrs. Peterson's tone like I do. Mother keeps her eyes on Mrs. Peterson, but deep grooves form on her brow.

"I can spare a bunch," Mother says. "But I'll accept no payment. There's as much grace in giving as there is in receiving. Rose, would you go to the garden, please? There's a rosebush among the chamomile that could do with a prune."

Frowning, I glance out the kitchen window. There aren't any rosebushes among the chamomile. Maybe Mother wants me to use my demigod power to grow a bunch of roses. I never have, but it would be the same as growing herbs. I leave the kitchen, but stop at the front door, realizing why Mother asks me to go outside.

She's going to hear Mrs. Peterson's secret. If I've angered Harpocrates, *I* should hear the secret and prove I'm committed to his cause. I don't want to live in a world without hope. I was angry earlier because I don't want to be disposable.

"Mother," I say, turning around. "Could you point out the rosebush? I'm not sure which one you mean."

When Mother joins me in the doorway, I lower my voice to a whisper. "Let me hear her secret."

Mother frowns. "I'd rather you didn't. I don't like the feeling I get from Mrs. Peterson."

"Please, Mother. I know she might have a terrible secret, but I can help her, I know I can."

Mother sighs. "Very well." She looks back at Mrs. Peterson. "I'll return in a moment. Rose will keep you company while you wait."

When Mother goes outside, I hurry back to the kitchen and sit at the table. Mrs. Peterson smiles with indifference and gazes about our kitchen. I wonder how I'll engage her in conversation, when it's clear she has no interest in talking to a teenager.

"I love the color of your dress-suit," I say. "The blue is the same shade as a periwinkle flower." I don't know why I thought of that flower when there are so many others to choose from. The periwinkle is also called the 'flower of death'. The vines were used in wreaths for dead children.

"It's my favorite," Mrs. Peterson says, "but its wool-blend is a poor choice of wardrobe in our current weather."

The umbrella didn't stop the rain soaking her clothes. Her dress-suit gives off a damp animal smell. The rain ruined her makeup, too. It's splotchy in places, especially around her left cheek. Wondering why she applied so much makeup during wet weather, I stand and fetch a towel so she can pat herself dry.

"Appearances must be important to your husband if he sends you out for flowers in dismal weather," I say, handing her the towel.

Mrs. Peterson flinches. "When you live in the public eye, appearance is a necessity, not a luxury." She pats her neck dry, then sips her tea. "The tea is delicious. Peppermint?"

"Yes. Infused with ginger. For your sniffles. I'm sorry to sound rude. I sense something troubles you. It helps to talk, did you know?"

She lowers the cup to the table. "You'll find out, young Rose, that even if you had someone to talk to, some things can't be helped."

"I imagine it would be difficult to find someone to trust when you live in the public eye," I say, sliding into my seat. "But you can talk to me. I can keep a secret."

"Can you now?" she says. "What on earth makes you think I have a secret?"

"I sense it. I also feel it troubles you."

She gives me a tired smile. "You're a strange, sweet child, and I appreciate the sentiment. If you must know, it's a demanding job meeting my husband's expectations. I'll say no more on the matter, but I trust you'll never repeat this conversation."

"You can trust me," I say. "But if you don't confide in somebody, the burden your secret causes you now will haunt you three times worse in death."

"There's more to fear in life than in death, young Rose," she says, ruefully. "If being haunted is the price I'll pay for holding my tongue, then so be it."

She returns to gazing about the kitchen, dismissing me completely. I wonder if I've wrecked the opportunity to cast my charm by being too forward. I need to hold her hand, but doubt she'll welcome the consoling gesture. But her manicured fingernails gives me an idea.

"I've never applied nail polish," I say, "but if I did, what color would you recommend?"

Extending my arm across the table, I offer my hand. Mrs. Peterson looks down her nose at my fingers, but then takes my hand in hers and studies my nails.

"Nothing too bold," she says, tilting my hand from side to side. "I prefer pale pinks or pearl, or there's a lovely shade of ivory I've used..."

She prattles on about the best color for teenage girls, remarks on my ring, picks at my nails and advises how best to shape them. While she talks, my charm wraps around our hands, binding us as one. Then it goes in search of her secret. It feels like forever, but in less than a second, images fill my mind. The charm has found the secret, but it's so shocking, I nearly jerk my hand away—

She's not the happily married wife of the hardworking town mayor. She's the victim of a cruel and calculating narcissist. Her self-esteem has suffered because of his controlling and abusive behavior, and years of verbal and physical abuse have left her a broken woman. With her sense of self-worth corrupted, she's lost view of a life away from her husband. She believes that what she endures behind closed doors is her lot in life.

To learn she's a victim of marital abuse staggers me. It explains the other images that fill my mind. She applies extra makeup to cover a bruise on her cheek. She cowers before her enraged husband because the color of her dress didn't match his tie. Her desperate need to find roses is born from a need to keep her husband happy; protection against his abuse.

I fuel the charm with hope drawn from an image of a blue sky after a clearing storm. The charm whips around Mrs.

Peterson's conscience. It removes a thick layer of hopelessness and replaces it with hope. Then it carries the hopelessness back to me.

"If you need more advice," Mrs. Peterson says, releasing my hand, "my nail technician has a shop near to the town hall. Mention that I sent you." She picks up her cup, pauses, then drinks the rest of her tea. When she lowers her cup, her sniffles have dried and her eyes shine with hope.

"Such an extraordinary taste," she says, smacking her lips with pleasure. "It's left me wonderfully clear-headed. I must take some with me."

"Of course." Going to the kitchen bench, I fill a paper packet with a mixture of dried ginger and peppermint leaves. Mrs. Peterson's hopelessness affects my usual care when preparing herbal tea, and I spill leaves on the bench.

Clenching my fingers, I take a deep breath and draw on my charm's power to help keep my emotions balanced. I don't know how Mrs. Peterson managed for so long, living without hope. Praying I gave her enough, I fold the packet and return to the table.

Mother arrives, holding a bunch of red and white roses that fill the kitchen with a heavenly scent. Feeling the hopelessness creep over me again, I catch Mother's eye and signal my desperate need to leave.

"Your roses," Mother says, her tone clipped.

Mrs. Peterson picks up her purse and stands. "Wonderful. And the tea?"

I hand her the packet. "A gift," I say when she opens her purse to pay.

Mrs. Peterson closes her purse and takes the packet. She looks me in the eye, as though reminding me never to repeat our conversation, then turns toward the door.

Mother escorts her out. "The rain has eased," she says, "but mind your speed while driving. The road into town is slippery when wet."

As soon as Mrs. Peterson leaves, I push past Mother and run to the garden. Dropping to my knees, I sow Mrs. Peterson's secret into the mud. The flooded soil reflects the charm's golden glow. When all Mrs. Peterson's hopelessness has drained out of me, I roll back on my heels and watch the secret grow.

A stem pushes through the ground, tall and thick with long thorns that droop as though they've lost the will to live. The rosebud that blooms at the top unfurls blood-red petals, with perfume so heavy it gets caught in my throat.

Standing, I stare at the rose. I'm supposed to listen without judgment, but I can't ignore what I heard. Mrs. Peterson faces more harm if she doesn't reveal her secret. The hope helped clear her mind, but will it be enough to encourage her to seek help?

I toss and turn all night, unable to get Mrs. Peterson off my mind. Thinking about her bruised cheek makes me lie awake with worry. Even if I broke my vows and revealed the secret for her, it wouldn't help. I'd destroy the hope I gave her, and she needs all the hope she can get.

Needing a slap of cold night air to clear my gloomy thoughts, I slip out of bed and go outside. The rain has stopped and the heavy clouds part, letting moonlight stream over the gardens. Taking a deep breath, I search the night shadows for Mrs. Peterson's rose. It's bathed a milky-white glow from the moon, but the light shifts as though moved by the wind. Wondering what causes that effect, I walk toward the rose. When I get closer, my heart stops.

It's not moving moonlight. It's the ghost of Mrs. Peterson. She hovers next to her wilted rose that's gray from death. Gone is the elegant woman who sat at our kitchen table. An unnatural force squishes her features, making her look like a lump of melted wax.

I stare at her, frozen in fright. How could I miss the signs that foretold her death? I compared the color of her dress-suit to the 'flower of death'. Mother warned her about the slippery roads. Did she have a car accident while driving home? Whatever happened, despite the hope I gave her, she didn't reveal her secret. She can't have, because she suffers her burden in death.

Three-fold hopelessness pours like black ink from her hollow eye sockets. Her mouth yawns wide, expelling the choking scent of her rose. Nothing I envisioned comes close to what stands before me. But what if I'm to blame? What if, in my haste to cast the charm, I didn't give her enough hope?

"I'm sorry," I whisper, creeping toward her. "I don't know what happened, but you don't deserve to suffer in death when you suffered so much in life. I can help you. I can fix this."

Her soul now belongs to Hades, but I can still hear her secret and fill her soul with hope. It means Hades may lose his servant. And he'll demand my soul to compensate. But if I'm responsible for Mrs. Peterson's death, that's a consequence I'm willing to accept.

I think about all the things that give me hope and fuel the charm with so much power it shines like two suns. Then I reach for Mrs. Peterson's hands. Her fingers find mine, icy tendrils that numb my skin. A strange blue light flows into my charm, turning its golden light a frosty turquoise. With increased power, the charm whips around our hands, binding us as one.

Mrs. Peterson tilts my hand and pokes at my fingernails. Though distracted by the icy pricks on my fingers, I urge the charm to find her secret again. Powered by the blue light, it works faster than usual. In a split second, the secret I heard when sitting in the kitchen with Mrs. Peterson fills my mind again.

This time, the images are so lifelike they make me think I'm experiencing them. When her husband strikes her cheek, I flinch as though struck. But then a different image appears, a new secret—

Still alive but soaked from the rain, Mrs. Peterson walks up a spiral staircase. She clutches Mother's roses to her chest like a shield. Mr. Peterson stands on the top step, his face a furious shade of red. When she shows him the roses, he knocks them from her hands. Then he shouts that a wife who appears in public looking like a drowned rat will embarrass him.

Encouraged by the hope, Mrs. Peterson scoffs at his expectations. She says if he wishes to remain married, she'll decide if her appearance is appropriate.

Mr. Peterson strikes her face with a backhand that knocks her down the stairs. Her head hits the bottom step with a crack —

The flow of images ends as quick as her life did. Numb with shock, I try to fathom what I saw. Instead, I see Mr. Peterson again, but his features are fuzzy, like I'm looking through a transparent veil. I can see enough to know he's talking on the telephone. Hear enough to know what he said. *Slipped on the steps. A tragic accident.* Then the image fades.

The blood drains from my face, making me feel as cold as Mrs. Peterson. I can't see her eyes, but I can sense her somber stare. The truth about her death burns through the charm, and screeches of *"liar"* and *"murderer"* ring in my ears. It's Mrs. Peterson screaming, though her mouth is shut. Again she's been silenced, this time forever. But her husband can't silence me.

Determined to end her suffering, I urge my charm to remove all the burden. It's like scraping away layers of sludge, but, powered by the blue light, the charm collects it all. Then it delivers hope so pure, the brightness hurts my eyes. But I'm not prepared when my charm returns with the burden.

Triple the amount of hopelessness drags me to the pits of despair, draining my will to live. But my determination to see her husband punished for her murder anchors me to life. Pulling my hands from Mrs. Peterson, I stumble backward to escape the lure of death.

Filled with hope, Mrs. Peterson's grotesque features melt away. She appears as she did when she sat at our table, elegant, spirits lifted, and taking pleasure in sipping our tea. Then she fades, like mist dispersing in a breeze.

"Rose?"

Mother's voice drives the deadness from my limbs. Dropping to my knees, I dig into the mud and bury both of Mrs. Peterson's secrets. The ground around my fingers glows turquoise, my charm's new color. Two stems burst through the soil. They weave around each other like climbing vines, sprouting long black thorns that droop with three-fold hopelessness. Above my head, a rose blooms at the top of each stem. The petals on each are an unearthly frosty blue.

"Rose? What happened?"

The shock in Mother's voice sends tears streaming down my cheeks. "She's dead. Mrs. Peterson is dead."

Mother crouches beside me, her hand flying to her throat. "When? How?"

I claw my fingers into the mud, wanting to scream Mrs. Peterson's secrets into the night. Instead, I imagine Hades again, his expression smug, as though expecting me to break my vows. But if I do, I'll break Mrs. Peterson's trust and destroy the hope I gave her. That would be like killing her again.

Mother's words about finding the strength whisper through my mind, and I realize where my strength lies. Wiping my eyes, I clamber to my feet. "Mrs. Peterson didn't deserve to suffer in death. I heard her secret again, removed her burden and filled her soul with hope."

"And condemned yours." Standing, Mother grabs my elbow and pulls me away from the two roses. "What were you thinking, child? If Mrs. Peterson chooses rebirth, Hades will demand your soul to compensate. I warned you of this. Harpocrates will strip your ability to conjure hope to avoid a war with Hades."

Without hope, I'll lose my will to live and hand my soul to Hades by taking my own life. Even revealing Mrs. Peterson's secret wouldn't help. I'd destroy her hope and prevent her from being reborn, but Hades would still get my soul. I'd suffer the three-fold hopelessness I trapped in the thorns and I wouldn't survive that. But I can save my soul another way. There's something Hades and I have in common.

"Hades won't come for me," I say. "He values upholding vows above everything. And Mrs. Peterson can't be reborn because we are bound as one. While I live in this world, she'll stay in the underworld." In Elysium, where pure souls get sent.

I fiddle with my ring. The blue light that changed the charm's color has also turned the gold band a deep shade of turquoise. I've guessed the source of the blue light's power, but I don't think either god expected this. "Harpocrates could strip my powers so I can't conjure hope, but while I keep Mrs. Peterson's secret, I'll always have hope. Look." I hold out my hand and tease my charm from the ring. It jumps into my hand, a flickering bluish-gold flame.

"It's drawing hope from Mrs. Peterson," I say, "but that hope contains Hades' power, which is why it's so strong. Harpocrates would be a fool to abandon me now. With hope this powerful, we could win every battle against darkness and despair."

Mother doesn't look happy, but I've never been more certain. Like all the Secret Keepers before me, Mother included, my strength lies in the commitment to my vows. It means Mr. Peterson will escape punishment in this world, but he won't escape Hades.

I have to listen without judgment, but in the underworld, Hades' judges don't. When they judge Mr. Peterson' soul with the secret he keeps, they'll send him straight to Tartarus. I can't imagine a better punishment for a man who killed his wife.

See Pauline Yates's story "The Secret Keeper" online at Metaphorosis.
If you liked it, leave a comment. Authors love that!
Remember to subscribe to our e-mail updates so you'll know when new stories are posted.

About the story

"The Secret Keeper" developed from an idea I had for another anthology call back in 2019. The theme for that anthology was based around the Zodiac signs. Being a Taurus, I wanted to write a story that focused on Taurus strengths, with loyalty and trust at the top of my list. I penned the original version, but put it aside to work on other projects because I needed more time to think about how best to show the traits I wanted to portray. The driving question behind the development of this story was this: What would the world look like if there was no one you could trust?

A year passed by the time I got back to it, and when I read over what I had, I thought it would be sad to waste the idea, so, with nothing else in the pipeline, I had another crack at it. As I've written for *Metaphorosis* before, I felt this story would be a good fit for what they like to publish. I submitted the first version of "The Secret Keeper" in October, 2020, but it was far different to the final published version. Despite much disarray in the world-building, the concept must have caught the publisher's eye because I was offered a rewrite opportunity.

Little did I know, it would take nine more versions, an extremely patient publisher, hours of research about Greek Mythology, and discussions with a church minister about the importance of vows, to pull together the finished version. My biggest issue was how to make demigod powers fit into the real world, because I was mixing the two. I've never written fantasy before, so this was more a challenge than I realized, but I am a fan of Percy Jackson and knowing how that world worked helped.

Ironically, every time I struck a hurdle, I'd find the answer. It was as though this story was begging to be told, and it was giving me all the clues. I just had to put them all together.

If you've read "The Secret Keeper", I hope you've taken from it the importance of staying true to your word. If you haven't read it, please consider doing so, especially if you keep a secret.

A question for the author

Q: Are you a Luddite? Or do you have the latest and greatest technology?

A: I don't like change. It's in my nature to immediately oppose any update to anything. It's not that I'm not open to improvement, rather I'm an 'if it's not broken, don't fix it' person. For example, while everyone spent the last ten years updating their phones to smart phones, iPhones, Androids, I stuck with my Samsung flip phone. All I could do was make a phone call and send a text, but that's all I needed. I always managed to find a way around the need for carrying a 'computer in a purse'. I had to buy an android phone last year, but only because I couldn't find another flip phone, when my old one finally died. And yes, I love it now that I'm used to it, but it got yelled at a few times in the learning process. It's the same with my laptop. It took me two years to convince myself to buy a laptop for my writing, and it's still the only one I've ever owned. It's twelve years old, had three hard-drive replacements, and I'm still running the 2007 version of Word. Will I update? Not until my laptop breathes its last breath. Do I feel behind the times? Nope. Until my situation changes and I need something flashier, I'm happy to keep things as they are. If the worst happens, there's always pen and paper, of which I have plenty.

About the author

From Queensland, Australia, Pauline Yates likes to explore the 'improbable' through her writing. When she's not burning the midnight candle researching her ideas, she loves watching movies that pit humans against nature, debates with anyone who'll listen about how dystopian societies start, and argues with her ancient cat about his demand to be fed at 3am. She also enjoys taking photos of the sunrise, if she wakes up in time.

paulineyates.com, @midnightmuser1

Satyajit Ray's Beard or the Lack Thereof

Abhijato Sensarma

"And why would there be multiple Earths in the same universe?" the counsellor asks me. She's not *my* counsellor—and this isn't my world. But she still has the same pair of spectacles resting on the bridge of her nose, and she peers through them to look at me. She must have been confused at the start of today's discourse. Usually, we talk about my marriage being in the wrong place, not my body being on the wrong planet.

I slip forward on the sofa. The woman sitting beside me looks at me with concern —but now that she's out of my line of sight, I can think better. It took me some time to accept the fact that she's my wife in this world. She has a shaved head here, but what truly took me by surprise was the fact that we were sleeping in the same bed when we woke up. And when I told her I shouldn't be there, she looked at me with an expression of love for me which I did not know she still allowed herself to reveal.

When I first came here, I did not know what to expect—in many ways, I still don't. But my professional life's turned out to be the same as it's always been. I'm still a quantum engineering professor. I'm still working on teleportation. And I still *feel* like myself—I'm a resident of my own mind, at the very least. But there're two big differences in this world that set it apart from mine.

"If the shape of the universe is flat enough, as evidence seems to suggest, then it's constantly expanding." My hands spread outwards in front of me as I start my monologue. It's a habit I have. "And if molecules are allowed to arrange themselves in every way they can over infinite space, they'll eventually run out of unique combinations. Patterns will start repeating—and the same worlds will arise in different parts of the universe."

The counsellor nods again. She steals the slightest of glances at my wife between looking up from her notebook and looking at me—"Have you considered the possibility ... that this may be a reaction to your wife having cancer?"

I bend my head sideways, confused. Couples therapy has never been my favourite part of the weekend, but neither has the counsellor ever been this wrong. She thinks I'm going crazy.

My wife's bald head steals my attention more than her eyes. But oh, her eyes do read of pity. I don't want any.

"*My* wife isn't dying from cancer." I say it with an emphasis on my baritone. It sounds harsh, almost dismissive. *You're in denial*, the counsellor seems to think. But once again, she doesn't say anything. She simply brings up her arms to the handrest on her seat and leans on it, thinking of how to approach this case.

Just then, the alarm clock in her room goes off. She snaps her fingers and mutters "*Turn est.*" A switch moves by itself, and the alarm stops ringing. "Time's up, so that will be all for today. I think we're making real progress here so far. Same time, next week?"

She smiles at me, but I retain my nonchalance. I stare at the portrait of Satyajit Ray in the background—he's the most revered filmmaker in Bengali cinema. But here, he has a beard akin to a Tagore, whereas Ray was famously clean-shaven in my own world. This isn't my home. And this isn't the Ray whose films I've grown up watching.

The portrait shouldn't even be there— in my world, the counsellor hung her framed diploma on this wall, so that it would be facing us during the session. But in the strange new place I find myself in, the diploma's on the other side of the wall, where Ray's portrait should have been. It's a reversal which doesn't say much, except that this isn't my world to inhabit.

I look at the woman who claims to be my wife. As a way of compensation for my harshness, she says to the counsellor, "Thank you, Doctor." Then, she mutters something under her breath. I don't catch the spell this time around. She's intentionally using the tone she always does when she's cross with me. And before I can do anything about it, a white beam of energy envelops her. By the time the energy dissipates, so does she. I'll find her at home again.

"Umm," I say, looking around the room. I run my fingers over the leather on the sofa with my left hand, and run the other hand across my hair. "I guess ... I'll just walk back home."

I nod awkwardly at the counsellor and pat my thighs before getting up. She looks at me with concern that brims over to amusement. She doesn't say anything, of course—but she's only human.

The counsellor's the least of my concerns as I walk down the stairs and make my way onto the road. The *autorickshaws* and taxis converge in the middle of the four-way intersection, pausing for a moment when the signal opens for the other side. Soon, their turn comes as well. I stand and stare at them for a while, until all the vehicles I tried to keep track of have disappeared out of sight. There isn't too much of a difference between the public transportation of the Kolkata I know and the one I'm in right now, except for the fact that all vehicles hover above the ground here. They have no wheels, but they do have drivers and an automated gear shift technique that does not require the assistance of hands.

I've learned about it on the Internet, which is no less fascinating or abusive than the one I know from my own planet. I'm a product from before the World Wide Web's time, but the evolution of science seems to have followed a less stringent path on this world, where magical spells do a lot of what science and maths account for in mine. I don't like this place.

It's been less than twenty-four hours since I found myself in this world, but in that time, I've come to understand that the most commonly used spell is the one which helps in transportation. People don't use it all the time, and prefer using public vehicles when they can—it's akin to not taking a helicopter every time you want to cross the street, I guess. But the spells used here are strange, as spells have always been. They're spelled in Latin, as well. What *is* the one for transportation, though?

I try saying it out loud. "Trans— transvec—*transvectio—*"

And just as I pronounce the spell—it's the correct one, it seems—I find myself disintegrating. It's a strange sensation, and I would think about it more if not for the fact that my mental facilities seem to be incapacitated. When I feel complete again, with my senses and my cognitive abilities returning, the first thought I have is—"What on Earth?"

It's an ironic choice of words considering my situation. I find myself looking straight at Satyajit Ray's bearded portrait again. According to the *Basic Dictionary of Magic*—whose online website I accessed yesterday—one's always transported to the place they're thinking about at the time of saying the spell. Using this spell effectively is an acquired habit.

I look down, and there is the counsellor again, peering over her spectacles and straining her neck with curiosity no longer censored by the hours she's being paid for. I see a notepad on her lap. She's probably filing away the minutes of today's session with us before the next client arrives.

"Hello ... What may I do for you?" She tries to wear a smile on her face, but her lips twitch back to a more neutral position.

I chuck my head to the right and smile, embarrassed at this intrusion of mine. "I've just transported myself to the wrong place when I intended to go back home. You see, I was thinking about your place

55

instead of mine, and I'm new to this magic business, so I didn't realise what would happen if I said *transvectio—*"

And just then, I can't feel my toes again. I realise what's going to happen next—*I've spoken the spell, haven't I?* But before I can think too much about the nuances of transporting for the second time in as many minutes, I'm no longer able to feel my thoughts either. It's serene, almost meditative, to not carry the worries of these worlds on my shoulders.

But when my feet touch the ground again, I throw up. It's on a familiar rug— the one I brought back home after spending a year in Switzerland working on the effects of extreme altitudes on my teleportation machine. The machine never worked. And in this world, it doesn't need to.

"Hey," I hear the familiar voice say. It's my wife's, even if it's mellowed down now. Probably because of the cancer. And also, because her husband seems to have gone crazy.

I look up at her. She's in her robes, getting ready for a bath. But before I can tell her anything—or apologise as a way of coming to terms with the place that is going to be my home for the rest of my life

—I feel my eyes closing. I didn't even say a spell this time. *Where am I going now?*

But before I can take in my new surroundings, my face hits the floor. The first—and last—thought I have here is that my nose is going to hurt like hell when I wake up again.

On opening my eyes, I see the roof above my head. I can still hear the public vehicles making their way past our home on this main road of the city. I never liked this place, even though the apartment itself is fine. Furnished at the time of purchase too. It's just that the commotion of the bazaar and the cars have never been to my liking. On the other hand, my wife thought the familiar sirens and rhythmic honks which compose this room's overtones would give me comfort when I came back home after the uncertainty of conducting experiments at my laboratory. I didn't think it would help, but over time, the sounds of the street have indeed turned meditative for me.

I find a reflection of my life in the taxis which pick up their passengers below at inflated rates. You can bargain, you can curse, and you can go anywhere you want —but at the end of the day, the taxi always drops you off at home. You've seen the sights of the city, yet there's the same old bed you need to sleep on. Beside a woman you loved once, but now can't bear to touch.

She realises I'm awake, though, and moves into my field of vision. I still don't want to touch her, because she isn't mine to have, and she isn't mine to love. But even if she were, would I want to? I feel uncomfortable about the realisation that she's a mortal—in both this world, and the one I've come from.

Before I can grasp at the finer ends of this chain of thought, I'm brought back to reality by a sudden pang of physical discomfort. My eyes look down, and I can see the bridge of my nose—it's certainly not where it should be. It's bent way too much towards my right. It's on the verge of being numb, but isn't, which makes the pain intolerable now that my senses are fully returning.

This wife moves her fingers and says a spell which does not penetrate the ringing sound in my ears. But the sound eventually dissipates, and as it does so, I feel my nose align itself properly. It almost twitches—no, it *jumps* back into its place.

I want to move away from her, for no fault of her own. She reminds me of my own wife too much—the one with whom disagreements have turned into silent nights. But even now, when she seems as foreign to me as she's ever been, I cannot stop admiring her. She always was the more tenacious of us. During separation or a bout with cancer, how does she remain the pleasant one?

She looks at me now with a love in her eyes I did not know I'd been missing. A love which is unconditional and comes out in moments of solidarity that have not yet turned into gestures born out of obligation.

But I cannot allow myself to reciprocate the feeling, even if I feel a tinge of heartache. For, as much as I want to reach out now, and brush my hands against her hardened cheeks, she still isn't mine to love. So, I push my arms against the surface I'm lying on, attempting to get back up.

"No, you must rest. Have you forgotten about that time we went to Darjeeling and you transported twice in a minute?" The voice lets out a laugh, but she doesn't see it through. I've seen her do this before, but I realise now why she does it. We've hurt each other too much, you see, and expressing ourselves has become a luxury. A laugh about the good old times has long been replaced by a few more moments of silence in my world.

"What happened to me? Am I a serial fainter in this world?" The weather's always been oppressive in this part of the country during the summers.

"You've got the Paralysis Syndrome, or have you forgotten that as well?" she asks. I shoot her a look. *I never knew*, I would like to tell her, but it wouldn't help.

Her head bows down as a way of resignation. "Your heredity means you can't teleport yourself like the rest of us can. You can only do it twice a day. You get quite tired otherwise. You pass out, like you did today."

I try to nod, but my head doesn't seem to be able to lift itself from the pillow for now. However, I do seem to recollect a stray line from the *Dictionary of Magic*'s entry about the subject. Something about people being born with a rare variation of the 24th pair of chromosomes, the ones that grant humans their ability to interact with magic. A pair which—in my world—is considered to lead to deformities and death rather than magical abilities.

"I ... I really might not be who you think I am."

She places a hand on her temple and looks away. "The mosquitoes are going to start entering the room again—let me shut the windows. *Prope.*" And on cue, the windows move inwards, as if they're intoxicated by a breeze blowing out of the room. The illusion of normalcy is shattered when the latches attached to the bottoms of the windows pick themselves up and lock them into their positions on the windowsills. Estranged or not, my wife remains cool across realms.

And right then, the first lines of Rabindra Sangeet burst through our closed windows, drowning out the noise of the receding vehicles as the last strains of sunlight drain away and the artificial lights take over. *"Ami chini go chini tomake, ogo bideshini." I know you, oh, I do, foreigner.*

Ah yes, I do. She's going to be my life now—there's no escape from it, and somewhere deep inside, I don't want there to be any. It will take time to learn this world's spells, perhaps, and it will take time to convince the counsellor that I was truly having a nervous breakdown about my wife's cancer today. But things aren't as bad with my wife here as they are back home. Our time together will be curtailed, but maybe I can learn to love her again all the same.

"Did I ever stop loving you?" I ask her, as a way of enquiring about the work I would need to put in to have a better relationship with her.

She shoots me another look. But I've always been this way, asking questions about love and existence while lying on the bed with a broken nose, if only figuratively. So, she answers, "No. As a matter of fact, ever since my diagnosis, you've loved me more than you ever have."

I try to nod, but it ends up looking like an awkward twitch of the head. She understands, though, and she laughs. For the first time in months, I'm able to smile with her. Oh, how I've missed that feeling of having someone there for me. The baggage of death takes precedence over marital discontent, I realise.

"Why does my nose ... feel normal?"

"I fixed it. It's the first spell you ever taught me. Transportation helped us get away from either of our parents if they saw us when they weren't supposed to.

You always landed on your nose whenever you fell unconscious. And I was always there for you. To fix your nose. Or just fix your hair."

So, in this world, I did find a way of escaping her parents. A less painful way than jumping out of her window from the first floor and breaking a bone in my leg that one time, for sure.

"Does this help you remember anything?" she asks.

"It does," I reply, remembering the exuberance of her youth—and mine—with a fondness I didn't think my marriage would still entail. "But then ... it doesn't." She sighs.

I've never believed in karma. Neither did I ever believe in magic before I saw it with my eyes. Perhaps this mystical experience of love I don't deserve is karma repaying itself for things I've done in lives I cannot remember. I would like to confess my sins to her, tell her how I've mistreated her.

But before I can, my wife rests her hands on my forehead. "You've become very tired because of this ordeal. Sleep now, and I'll sleep alongside you. Hopefully, you'll be in your senses when we wake up tomorrow. *Somnus.*"

And I feel myself drifting away again. I slip into oblivion, akin to how I've felt while teleporting before. But this time, I'm not reappearing to a different part of the world. My mind merely guides me to a world of my own. I feel a comfort I haven't felt for a long time now—the comfort of falling asleep next to someone you love.

"So, you believe you're from another dimension?" the doctor asks. I nod and look around the room. I see laminated certificates hanging where Satyajit Ray's portrait should be hanging. The portrait occupies the space on the wall right behind me. If I didn't know better, I would have thought the counsellor had just exchanged our seats as a way of giving the two of us a 'new perspective'.

But when I turn around to look at the portrait, Mr. Ray's likeness hangs up there without a beard on the man's face, as if it's a joke. His beard's the most iconic part of his appearance—and this world doesn't even have that. Alongside the fact that it believes magic exists only in escapist novels and ancient scriptures.

"Umm, yes, I do." I don't put in too much effort into my assertion, because I'm truly not interested in this session. This counsellor isn't the one I've been intimate with about my Paralysis Syndrome. And this wife isn't the one I've grown so close to because of her terminal cancer. She looks much younger sitting beside me now, untouched by fate or fear.

She loves me in this world as well. But she doesn't have terminal cancer—yet— and this makes her more placid, less lively, than my wife. The man who's actually married to her was the one who filed for divorce. On the other hand, my affection for her has turned platonic with the changing of worlds. I would like to embrace her, and apologise for the sins of another man, but I love her only as my confidant from a different life. It wouldn't be fair to love her any more than that.

She brought me in for an emergency counselling session today. She checked my temperature and cooked me a good meal first, even though I've become the one to do that in my own marriage back home. She cares for me, yes, she does—yet, as much as I care for this woman too, I can't seem to love her.

65

"*Have you considered that this could be related to the fact that the two of you want a divorce?*"

"*Ah,*" I say. "*It's the farthest thing from what I want, though.*"

My wife shoots me a look. "*You're the one who wanted it the most.*"

I get up from my place, and throw out my hands—it's a sign of desperation in this world too, I hope. "*I'm sorry, but this is all too much for me. Transvectio.*" I stand in my place, but nothing happens.

I'd forgotten. I don't have the chromosomes I need to perform magic in this world.

The counsellor bends her eyebrow at me. "*I've been learning a bit of Latin to cope with all this stress,*" I inform her. It's a trick I picked up at school, whenever anyone caught me practicing spells in an empty classroom or in a corner of the playground—I've never been good at magic. The excuse usually failed to protect me from the ridicule of my classmates when I was younger, but now, it helps me slip out of my unsuccessful attempt at teleportation.

I look around this familiar room set up in an alien manner for what I hope is the last time. "*I think I need a break. I'm*" unable to cope with the pressure, and I'd appreciate some space rather than being dragged down for therapy to this office. My apologies, I'll have to get going now." I do my best impression of storming out of the room and down the stairs of the large hospital. Theatrics, it turns out, will always convince others to leave an upset man alone, whether it has something to do with magical civilisations or not.

Some use the elevator, of course, but it's a relief to see most others walking beside me on the stairs. In my world, the presence of magic means people teleport themselves to the other end of a long journey in a matter of minutes. Everyone except for people like me, that is. On the other hand, everyone here needs to sit down and let a good old engine—and a decent driver—do the work instead.

As jarring as this reality has been to me so far, including the experiences with my very own wife, the biggest incentive for staying in this world has been the respect engineers are given here. In the society I've grown up in, engineering as a career has always been treated akin to a punchline. The electricity plants that power most of the world, the equipment that makes surgeries easier for Medical Wizards, and *of course, the transportation that helps the less biologically gifted ones among us—they're only possible with the help of scientists like us. But it's the Wizards who are at the helm of affairs. They're the most influential politicians and academics. They get to decide what others are known as. Many books have called the people of my profession an 'afterthought', replaceable tools only there to help the Wizards accomplish their goals. But society wouldn't be able to hold itself together if our kind disappeared overnight.*

This world, on the other hand, designs its fervour around supernatural elements of a different kind. I see the people praying in makeshift temples and on the rickshaws that carry models of their deities wherever they go. Not being treated as a dispensable labourer comforts me in a way I've never felt about my professional identity before. I wouldn't mind staying here—but I can't.

I've fought for a semblance of respect towards my profession for the longest time. It's the reason I started experimenting with manufacturing a teleportation device using scientific apparatus rather than relying on the genetic predispositions of the population. I've found what I've sought for all my life—but this isn't earned.

So, I make my way to the most familiar place I know after my home—the University I work at. The only difference being that here, the campus isn't guarded by magical sharks floating in the air.

Rather, the University's guarded solely by the same people I've become good acquaintances with back in my realm. It is closed off to students at this time of the evening, but when I flash my ID at one of the guards—a card which surprisingly does not morph itself into a miniature replica of its holder in this world—he lets me in. "Welcome, Professor," the man says, and steps aside.

I make my way up to the second floor. Room 616. *Here it is. I stand in front of the door for a moment, then another, and then another. It's on the last beat that I have to remind myself once more of the nature of human existence here. You've got to turn your own door handles in this world.*

I enter the room and switch on the lights. Here lies the machine. It looks the same. It's cylindrical, with a hollow, secured chamber in the middle of it large enough to fit a human—the place where the person must enter if they're to teleport.

This machine remains in its prototype stage, just like mine.

The most essential discovery I've made exists here too, in the form of a neutrino battery on top of the machine, powered by an alloy of platinum and plutonium. A 'radiation cover' ensures the battery is shielded and the machine can be dealt with in normal clothing. As a matter of abundant precaution, I slip on the gloves lying on the counter.

I proceed to open the chamber and look at the controls when I realise these gloves are not infused with any magical spells. This means that they aren't really protecting me from any radiation-related accidents. But I carry on. A preliminary inspection should not take long.

The machine looks the same on the exterior as mine. The keypad has an extensive entry system which allows for transportation to different parts of the Universe, even though this is an ambitious addition to the machine's infrastructure. It's purely theoretical, because it cannot function. Mine didn't, at least.

I pick up a screwdriver and unshackle the interior of the machine. Another cursory glance reveals what I've been suspecting ever since I entered this lab. The protoype, it turns out, is indeed a bit different looking here—on the inside! *I shift my focus away from the similarities and study the differences between my device and the one this Earth's version of me has created.*

I put on my protection kit and start with my work. I note down observations in my favourite notebook—this world's version of it, anyway. Blueprints lie all around my corner of the lab, and my suspicions are confirmed.

He's created one half of the machine, with his work delivering solutions to the long-drawn questions I've asked myself over the years during its construction. His configurations reveal things like how the neutrino battery should be wired to the quantum transportation engine, and whether I should add a circuit breaker before or after the feed from the electronic transmitted attached to the keypad is integrated into the CPU (before, of course, but only with a special modification to the industry model to make it compatible with my work). His notebook combines with my knowledge to show me the full picture, and thus, I can now complete this Teleporter to make it a functional one.

The switch must have happened yesterday, under the improbable conditions across both ends of the Universe where similar worlds created two polar opposites of machines which also had perfect compatibility with each other. The alignment of similar cellular structures did the rest, and the ambiguity in the positions of supercharged, hyperactive atoms altered the probabilities of their positions. This simultaneously attempted operation of compatible halves led to some sort of superimposition of the machine and its contents before the eventual separation. During this time, our consciousnesses must have switched—because while my body feels the same, it's lost the power to perform magic here—so it's likely his body. My counterpart probably has my former abilities, under this hypothesis.

But again, it's just that—a hypothesis. I can't remember for the life of me how I ended up tucked in bed on this world. I was a mess when I woke up in the morning. Maybe it's just the machine that does it. All I know is that the rest of my life seems perfectly stored in my mental faculties.

Such a freak accident probably won't occur again—neither the transportation, nor the memory loss—but it doesn't need to. I now know how to configure this *machine, and make it work from a single location. If I do manage to work things out soon, I can go home again, and help my other self out too.*

Let's see how I go about rescuing both versions of myself now—and inventing intra-dimensional teleportation along the way.

When I open my eyes, I expect to feel her palm on my forehead again, ready to put me to sleep if I haven't come around to what she thinks are my regular senses. Sunlight is peering in through the windows, which are open again, and carrying in the familiar hum of the vehicles during office hour.

I slide up in my bed and feel the sour taste in my mouth. I'll need to brush my teeth. What was the spell for doing that, again? *"Puriter lavit dentes." Have clean teeth.* It's the wordiest phrase I learned yesterday, but also the most convenient one of them all. I would also love to learn the spell which lets me floss, even though I've never done that as a regular human being before.

The brush should've been floating towards me with the perfect amount of paste on it, a proportion which no human hands could ever conjure. But it doesn't. I say the words louder. "*Puriter lavit dentes.*"

"Have you really been taking your Latin classes so seriously?" my wife asks. She'd been asleep, beside me. "I didn't realise you were taking any at all."

I turn towards her. Yes, I'm seeing *my* wife, because she has her long hair again. She's also got the beautiful smile and that radiance which comes from being optimistic about what life plans for you next.

And then, the memories come back to me in bits and pieces. I recollect the strange feeling with which I was greeted when I met another part of myself in a world which seems too distant to exist now.

He told me the theory he'd postulated, and introduced me to his machine—it was incomplete, yet revealed all I needed to know to get home. We worked on completing it overnight, and now, here I am, before the break of dawn. I can't recollect all the details, but I remember enough. He said he's noted down all that I would need in my notebook to construct another machine. I want to rush down to the University's laboratory to check if the memories I've retained aren't betraying me. And if there already is a fully functional Teleporter in my lab.

I remember his parting words as well. *Love your wife as much as you can, for as long as you can. Some of us don't have her for much longer—but then, neither will you, if you stop loving her.*

She still wears a look of confusion on her face, though, as she should. This is the first time in months that we've shared the same bed—I must have slipped in while she was asleep. She would have no way of knowing I've changed overnight, once again.

"Are you ... wearing a wig?" I ask.

Now, she shoots me the familiar look which indicates her confusion has been superseded by amusement. "I'm going to call the counsellor again. You could do with some medication—I didn't realise our divorce would get to you so much ..."

"You don't need to do that," I say.

Questions of science can wait—it's the ones of my heart that need to be answered first. In this world, *my* world, I realise that the two of us still have time. My wife's concerned. She's been concerned for the longest time, hasn't she? There's a tinge of sorrow which hides beneath her façade as well, but it's not of the inevitable kind. We can make things better between us.

"I've got another question," I say.

"What's it this time?"

"Did Satyajit Ray ever have a beard?"

"No, he was an indie filmmaker—not a crazy loon."

I break out into a smile. "I've been feeling like one myself up until now."

She tilts her head to the left.

I reach forward to caress her hair, and then I hug her for the first time in months —I didn't want to before, but now that I can, I wouldn't be having this any other way. She tries to move away at first, but then, she embraces me too.

We need to work on our relationship—a lot. But I'm in my own world again, in the arms of my own wife, and with an enriched Latin vocabulary. It isn't going to be easy. But the time to try isn't a luxury everyone has, unlike us.

I break away from our embrace for a moment. "I want things to be better. I want us to be happy again. And I don't want to leave you," I say.

"Neither do I."

"We can try again, can't we?"

She nods. Amidst the moments of silence yet to retreat from our relationship, I reach forward and embrace her once more. She's never stopped loving me, and now, I realise that neither have I.

See Abhijato Sensarma's story "Satyajit Ray's Beard or the Lack Thereof" online at Metaphorosis.
If you liked it, leave a comment. Authors love that!
Remember to subscribe to our e-mail updates so you'll know when new stories are posted.

About the story

I've always wondered—is it our circumstances that define us, or is it us who define our circumstances? There's no definite answer, but writing fiction has always been my way of debating the merits of different philosophies.

In this story, I wanted to explore how a fundamentally same person—across both worlds—lives vastly different lives. One's marriage is on the precipice of collapse; the other's wife is dying from cancer. One's career is well-reputed; the other's is much-maligned. A different social standing in life, then, might just be the result of circumstances beyond one's control. It calls for the lending of empathy, which we could all do with, especially during times like these.

In my home country of India, there remains a perception that science-related subjects are the most profitable as careers—and thus, the most important as well. Even the most educated people subscribe to this ideology, which simultaneously contributes to the disrepute of both Humanities subjects, as well as a pursual of the arts for a career.

I wanted to see how things would be from a different perspective. So, I focused on how an engineer might feel in an India where it wasn't them, but the wizards and witches, who would be setting the narrative. The answer circled back to my intent with this piece—all of us deserve empathy, for sometimes, our circumstances might be beyond us even when our fates aren't.

A question for the author

Q: What kind of non-fiction do you like to read and how does it affect the fiction you write?

A: I've always believed that fiction reflects reality in between its lines. The recognition of fundamental truths is what connects the author and the reader beyond the scope of a story's immediate facts. My favourite kind of non-fiction is sports writing. I've always been a cricket fan, and it's another medium where human stories shine through amidst all its unnecessary grandeur. I've learnt a great deal from the likes of writers like Jarrod Kimber, Andrew Fidel

Fernando, and Andrew Miller. The biggest lesson has been that telling a story is the primary job of all forms of writing, no matter what its purpose. This realisation has had quite an effect on me, and changed the way I deal with my craft.

About the author

Abhijato Sensarma is an 18-year-old student from Kolkata, India. He's on the verge of stepping into the real word, which does not prevent him from writing about fictional ones whenever he can. He's also been brought up on a steady diet of genre shows and books. So, even though he's expanded his horizons over the years, he still has an affinity for comforting stories. He dreams of becoming a professional writer —hopefully one who'll also retain the belief that art is the key to answering the mysteries of life.

@ob_jato

The Stranding

Maud Woolf

There's a sparrow lying on the crust of the snow, beak open, one wing folded. George watches it from a wary distance, gritting his teeth to keep them from chattering, hands shoved tightly up under his armpits. There's something strangely perfect about it, no blood or scattered feathers. But nothing living could be that still. It looks like someone's glove, dropped and forgotten. It must have died recently, to be left bare like that.

The snow was still falling when George went to bed last night. He left the curtains open to watch. The snowflakes were made orange by streetlamp light, sliding past the glass in hypnotic, patterned flurries.

This morning the snow is no longer alive, but still, as still and dead as the bird. Unsettled, George looks away, up at the house. This is a curtain-twitching kind of street in a curtain-twitching kind of village, but the windows are dark and empty.

Come on, he thinks. *Come on. Open the door.*

His toes are starting to ache, and he shifts from side to side, trying to stamp away the cold. He should just leave. He will leave. He doesn't need Tom to come with him.

Even so, something in his chest unwinds when the front door finally opens. He's taking a breath to yell at Tom for leaving it so long, when he sees it's Julia standing there in the doorway. He stops stamping and tries to smile.

"Oh, hi. I'm just waiting for your brother." He looks past her to the hallway, hoping maybe Tom is hiding behind her in the dark.

"I know," Julia says and then steps outside, shutting the door behind her. George feels his smile become a little more fixed. Talking to Julia alone always unnerves him. It's not just that she's a year older than him at twelve, or even that she's a girl, though in Tom's eyes at least that's enough to make her The Enemy. It's that George can remember a time before those things were important and it was just the three of them, having pretend adventures in the back garden. Julia had the best imagination out of any of them, telling them they were knights on a quest, superheroes, a wild pack of wolves. Nowadays, George can't look at her without remembering and feeling a squirmy kind of embarrassment.

"Is he coming out?" he asks. "Did he say?"

"Probably not," Julia says, kneeling on the step to lace up her hiking shoes. She's wearing a bright yellow puffer jacket that goes down to her knees, and when she stands up and zips it, she looks like a caterpillar. "He's still in his room."

"Well..." George says and lets out a huff of white cloud. "Can you tell him I'm here?"

"I did."

"Fucksake," George says but there's no heat in it. He knew really, even on his way over, that this was a pointless exercise. Tom hasn't answered his texts with anything more than single-word replies for a long time now. Still, George hoped that the message he sent Tom last night would have changed something. That knocking on Tom's door would have forced some kind of reaction.

"Sorry," Julia says, clearly not invested. She shoves her hands into her pockets and tilts her head to the side to look at him. It still reminds George of an owl, even if Julia's hair isn't short and tufty anymore. It's the same brown, but longer now and, George can't help but notice, greasy and unbrushed. There are purple shadows under her eyes and George wonders if she's only just gotten out of bed.

"It's fine," George says, scowling at his shoes. He wants to ask Julia to go inside and force Tom to come down, at least force Tom to *talk* to him, but that would be pathetic, so instead he just asks, "Where are you off to, then?"

He doesn't really care, but then Julia sniffs and juts out her chin. "With you. Thought I'd come and see what all the fuss is about."

"Tom told you where I'm going?" George asks. He tries to say it neutrally, but Julia must hear something in his voice because she scowls.

"Is it a secret?"

"No," George says, but then hesitates. "How much did he say?"

"He said you saw it fall." Julia says. "He said you're going to find it."

She says it bluntly, but that's nothing new for her. Julia doesn't act like the other girls he knows, who were always in groups, whispering and giggling behind their hands. When George saw Julia at school she was almost always alone.

Sometimes when Tom talked about Julia, his anger sounded wounded, as if she had betrayed them by growing up and becoming a girl. As if she had defected to the enemy side. George would never say it, but he finds this hard to believe. Julia doesn't seem to belong to any side at all.

George looks down and kicks at the snow a little with the toe of his boot. "He's talking, then?"

"Not a lot. I had to force it out of him," Julia says. Then she clears her throat and says, more brusquely, "It's not going to stay light for long. How far is it?"

"Er, not that far, but I'm not sure that..."

"Are we walking?"

George hesitates, aware that he's losing control of the situation. Tom was always the one to tell her to *Go away, no girls allowed*, but Tom isn't here and without him it's hard to remember why it's so important to stay away from Julia anyway. He imagined today with Tom there at his side, but now, when it comes to it, maybe anyone would be better than going alone.

He just shrugs, in the end.

"I was going to cycle some of the way. You could borrow Tom's bike, maybe?"

"I don't know how."

"Right," George says heavily. He looks over at his bike.

"I'm not riding on the back," Julia says quickly. "I'll fall off."

George sighs and resists the temptation to point out he hadn't offered. "Okay. I guess we're walking then. Can I lock this to the fence?"

He doesn't wait for the answer, pulling off his glove with his teeth to fumble numbly at the lock. His finger slips and he swears, muffled by a mouthful of wool. Last night, with his head stuck out of the window, snow falling in his hair while he waited for the sirens, this plan was exciting, almost perfect. Now, it's beginning to feel like a mistake.

With the bike secured, he walks back over to Julia, who is looking down at the sparrow with an unreadable expression.

"It must have flown into a window," he says, wondering if she might suggest they bury it or something. He doesn't remember her ever being very sentimental. The stories she had made up for them were always violent. When they were pirates, she had George walk the plank by bouncing off the trampoline. He misjudged the jump and as he lay winded on the grass, Julia had circled him, saying, *The sharks smell blood. Did you feel that one touch your leg?*

"They're not always dead," is all she says now. "Sometimes they're just stunned."

"It looks dead."

"Yeah," she says, frowning. "Yeah, I think it is."

George clears his throat. "So, should we, ah...?"

"We can go."

She doesn't say it like a command, but when they start walking, he makes sure to go in front. This is, after all, his expedition.

It doesn't take them more than ten minutes to reach the outskirts of the village and start cutting their way over the farm track that runs between the fields. George spends the time trying to think of something, anything, that they can talk about. Even back when they were little, it was always the three of them together. Without Tom, George doesn't know how to act around her. Julia makes no effort to fill the silence and George doesn't know if she feels the same way or if this is who she is now, this quiet, withdrawn person. In all his memories, she's talking.

The air feels muffled now that the wind has died down, and the clouds feel very close overhead, like big balls of cotton pressing down on them. It's quiet enough that the crunching noise of their footsteps feels startling. He can hear Julia struggle for breath as the track gets steeper and it makes him too aware of his own breathing, taking in air through his nose even though the cold of it hurts.

He can't help but keep checking over his shoulder in the hopes that Tom will pop up in the distance, a dark shape running to catch up.

The fourth time he does it, Julia makes a face. "No one's going to care that we're going."

"I know," George says, feeling defensive. "I'm not worried about that."

He is, though, just a little, but only out of habit. Technically, everyone is meant to stay in their houses for a full twenty-four hours after the sirens go off. A year ago, there might have been policemen about, even all the way out here in the countryside. There was a hotline you could call to report on your neighbors if you saw them out on the street.

No one cares much these days. Streets stay empty anyway. There are a few tattered posters left on lampposts, warning people of the dangers of contamination, but the policemen have all gone. George doesn't know if this is because they're needed elsewhere or if there are just fewer and fewer of them.

Sometimes he thinks they've just stopped trying. Go outside or don't, it doesn't seem to matter. The same thing happens to everyone.

The sirens are the only constant, and George finds them almost comforting now. It means that someone, somewhere, is setting them off. Someone is still watching the sky and waiting with their finger on the button.

It's a relief when they finally reach the ragged treeline. When he looks back over his shoulder, the village has already shrunk down into the crook of the valley. It looks like a handful of toy buildings left out on a dirty white carpet. It looks like nothing at all from here.

"Which way now?" Julia asks, peering dubiously into the gloom. George hates to admit it, but she was right to worry about losing daylight. At this time of year, it is pitch black by teatime.

"West."

Julia snorts. "I'll get out my compass, shall I?"

"Up the hill," he says begrudgingly. "That way."

Julia doesn't step forward, frowning up at the trees, and George wonders suddenly when she last left her house. The village isn't large, and he thinks he knows all the people left. He's come across them from time to time, walking aimlessly like him. Sometimes they nod at each other or even stop to talk, but he's never seen Julia. Every time he passed Tom's house, the windows were dark and empty. Was she inside the whole time?

"Do you want to go back?" George asks her.

He tries to say it gently, but Julia sniffs, offended, and shakes her head. "No. But you're leading the way."

It's dark under the trees and they have to watch their step to avoid tripping on the roots. George is going first and when he pushes back a branch, he holds it to let Julia through.

The damp chill of the bark seeps through his gloves and he shudders, wrinkling his nose at the smell of rotting leaves. He's spent most of the last year going on long rambling walks with his headphones jammed in, but he's not an outdoors person by nature. Still, anything is better than watching television alone in the living room, pausing every time there's a creak from the floor above, imagining that maybe it's his mum and dad, that maybe they will come downstairs showered and dressed and smiling. *Enough lying about*, his dad might say, *I'm starving. Who wants breakfast?*

"Very chivalrous," Julia says drily as she pushes past.

You're welcome, George thinks darkly, but contents himself with scowling at the back of her bright yellow hood.

They walk in silence for a while and then out of nowhere she says, "He wanted to come along. Tom did, I mean."

"So why didn't he?" George asks, batting a leaf irritably out of his face.

"He's not...he doesn't leave his room much these days. Mum and dad too."

George is silent for a moment and then, because he can't stop himself, because he has to tell someone, he admits, "Mine don't either."

"For how long?" She doesn't sound surprised. She doesn't even look back, for which George feels strangely thankful.

"I don't know," he says. "Dad started getting quieter from the very start, the first fall. But mum was okay till last week."

"It comes on fast," Julia says. "I thought I would see it coming after mum and dad, but with Tom I thought he would be okay. I thought maybe it wouldn't happen to him. I thought..."

Her voice wobbles and she doesn't finish. George doesn't know what to say. For a moment it's too much, the frustration, the hopelessness of it all. He stops walking.

"Tom was fine," George says and to his horror the words come out thick and heavy. "Just a month ago. He was *fine.*"

Julia stops then and looks back over her shoulder, and George thinks she's going to make fun of him, stamping his feet like a little kid, talking about how unfair it all is. Or worse, she might try to be kind. It would be wrong, George knows, for Julia to try and comfort him.

Tom is her brother after all, not his.

To his relief, she just nods, face tight and drawn.

"I just wish..." he starts and then, feeling stupid, he looks down at the mud on his shoes. "I just wish we could do something."

"We are, though," she says. "We're going to find the angel."

For a moment they look at each other in silence and then George nods.

"Yeah," he says. "Yeah, you're right."

"We should get on, then." Julia smiles at him. It's crooked and a little awkward, like she's not used to it, but George tries to return it as best he can.

"Yeah." He scrubs a hand over his nose, sniffs and sets off again, moving faster now. Soon he'll have to pull out the map and check the marking he made last night and the thought of that is comforting. This could still be what he wanted it to be last night. An adventure.

"You don't think they're aliens, then?" he asks when they're a little further on. He's speaking too loudly, he knows, but he's embarrassed to have almost been caught almost crying in front of her. Even when they were both kids that would have been shameful.

"Maybe they're aliens. Maybe aliens and angels are the same thing."

"You don't care?"

"I don't think it's important. If someone knows, then they won't tell us, but I don't think anyone does know."

"I think they know," George says quickly. "I think there's a reason they're not telling us."

"Oh yeah? Why's that?"

George can't see her face, but he can tell she's making fun of him. He doesn't care. He's spent too long staring at his computer scrolling through message boards and the itch to share his research wins out. It's not like anyone else is asking him.

"I think it's because they did it. It's their fault. The satellites sent out some kind of frequency that's poisonous to these things. Like whales."

"Whales?"

"The way our sonar messes with their echolocation and they beach themselves. That's why they're coming here. They're confused."

"Hmm. And who are *they*?"

George looks back over his shoulder, confused, and then nearly trips. "Huh?"

"They," Julia says. "With the capital T. The people doing this."

George sighs and tries to control his rising frustration. They talked about this on the message boards too, the way nobody seemed to care. George cares. Sometimes it feels like the questions are the only thing left in his head.

"The   government,"   he   says. "Companies."

"What   companies?"   Julia   asks. "McDonalds? Facebook?"

There's no bite to it, but George doesn't want to play this game anymore.

"You asked," he says and then stops and makes a big show of taking out his map and compass so that she'll see he's not   interested   in   continuing   the conversation.

She looks over his shoulder at the map and, as if to make amends, she hums in a way that could be called impressed. "It's close. How did you work out where it fell?"

"I saw it. Last night."

She raises her eyebrows. "From your window? What did it look like?"

For some reason, George doesn't want to tell her. The memory feels private. His face was so close to the window that the skin of his nose went rubbery and cold from the glass. He was looking for it, but even so, the hair on the back of his neck stood up when it came into view. It only lasted a moment, but for some reason in George's memory it took a long time to fall. The storm must have been at its peak, but he remembers it being silent, so silent he could have sworn he heard his heart beating in his chest. Too fast. Like it wasn't his heart at all. Like a bird's heart.

"It looked like a star," he says. "A shooting star."

Julia hums. "I guess that makes sense. It was burning up in the atmosphere."

"Maybe," George says. The thought makes him strangely uncomfortable.

"I hope there's some left and it's not just a melted burnt-up lump." She must see the look on his face because she laughs. "Sorry, was that too gross?"

"Yes," George says shortly and sets off again at a brisk pace.

He's expecting, no, *hoping* for silence now, but if anything, Julia seems to have been cheered up by his increasingly bad mood.

"It isn't a bad theory," she says. "Your one. But how does it explain the fallout?"

"The fallout?"

"You know," she says. "The sadness."

"I don't know. I read something about it just being like shock. Of first contact." The article he read put it more scientifically than that, but George just skimmed it.

He doesn't care so much about that part. That part is too real. That part is his parents sleeping for twelve hours a day. Not talking for the rest.

"If I did think it was angels," Julia says, so quietly he almost misses it. "Then that would be evidence, I think."

"Why?"

"I don't know. It feels like a... I don't know... a spiritual sickness."

When George looks back, her cheeks are pink, and she won't meet his eyes.

"I guess," he says but it's dubious. His own parents aren't very religious, but he's seen the Bible in Tom's living room.

"Well what do you think it is? Radiation or contamination or whatever?"

"Well that's what they say," George says darkly.

Julia laughs. "Oh, *them*. At it again."

"Well it's a good excuse isn't it? For the sirens? For keeping us inside for twenty four hours, for not letting us get close?" He's riled up again, he can feel his face getting warm but for some reason it feels strangely good to be angry. "They just want to hide the evidence."

"Maybe you're right," Julia says slowly, like she's turning something over in her mind. "That would almost be nice, wouldn't it? If it were their fault. I think that would be easier."

They're both silent after that.

As the ground rises, the trees start to draw more tightly in around them. More than a few times they have to change direction in order to get around some tricky patch of undergrowth. This makes George increasingly nervous, and every ten minutes he makes them stop and check the map. It's only a little past midday, but already the light is changing, the trees losing detail, stiffening into stark silhouettes.

The edge of the forest comes without warning. There is no slow sparsening of trees. One moment they are picking their way carefully through the gloom and in the next they are stumbling out into bright emptiness.

Ahead of them, the ground veers sharply up to the bald head of the hill. The snow is thicker up here, and the wind snatches at their clothes, looking for gaps between glove and sleeve, scarf and collar. The skin of his face feels pinched.

"I didn't realize we were so high up," Julia says. Her voice sounds thinner out here, lost in the new space that has opened up around them. It felt better somehow, to only see the sky in gaps between branches.

"Let's get to the top," George says, teeth chattering. "I think we'll see it from there."

He doesn't step forward. They've come all this way. He could move if he wanted to. He should want to. He did want to.

We'll see it from the top of the hill. The thought feels sick, suddenly. Wrong.

George clears his throat. Maybe it would be okay to turn back now. Maybe they don't need to go any further. He wants somehow to convey this to Julia, but the words won't come.

"Julia," he says. "What if I was wrong? What if it *is* dangerous, to get too close to it?"

Hearing himself say it, he sounds childish and stupid. Maybe he should have stayed home, done as he was told. Maybe they were telling the truth, maybe there is no conspiracy after all, nothing hidden. Maybe it's no one's fault.

Julia looks over at him, her eyes pale above the red blotches on her cheeks. "It might be. But we're already here," Julia says. "And the worst that can happen is we end up like the others."

Something about the way she says it sounds almost wistful, and George has a sudden impulse to reach out and take the sleeve of her yellow coat, pull them both back under the trees.

"Do you want that?" he asks. "Why did you want to come here?"

"Same as you," she says. "I need to do something."

She opens her mouth and closes it and then, as if she can't help herself, she keeps going, the words coming out in a messy rush.

"It's too late for our parents and too late for Tom and maybe for you and me too. But I have to see it for myself. I have to *know*."

She looks at him like she wants him to understand and George thinks of her looking down at the bird, with that strange expression on her face. He didn't understand at the time what it meant. He thinks of her alone in that quiet house and he thinks of her listening, like him, hoping for the creaking floorboards.

"You can wait here," Julia says. "I'll look and come back."

She says it simply and without judgement, and George remembers all at once that the story didn't stop with the sharks biting at his toes. He remembered Julia looking up, widening her eyes and pointing, saying, *What's that on the horizon?*

Tom had been rolled over on a skateboard, reaching out his hand, with Julia calling out, *A raft, a raft, Tom's here to save you*, but even then George knew it wasn't Tom who rescued him, that it was Julia who took pity on him, Julia who saved him from drowning. He loved her for it then, and now he thinks that maybe it isn't embarrassment that makes his stomach twist when he sees her now, but guilt. Because Julia saved him and kept the sharks away and then he grew up and abandoned her for it.

"I'm going," George says. "I want to see it too."

It's suddenly very important that neither of them should be alone.

Julia looks at him for a moment, and whatever she sees in his face seems to bring her to a decision, because she nods and turns to go, head tilted upwards towards the ascent. George follows close behind, stumbling a little in the snow.

Walking is harder now, much harder, and with every step the snow drags at his feet. The climb gets steeper and steeper but somehow the hilltop seems to remain in the same place, always just out of reach. Twice he stumbles, and on the third time he falls forward onto his knees. Julia turns back, eyes too large in her head, but George waves her away, gets up. The fall was painless, but the wet seeps through his trousers and, even through the glove, his hand feels raw where he caught himself against the snow.

Everything is shades of white, the sky dirtied and yellowish, the ground like bone, and in the middle of it all is Julia in her yellow coat, always just a little ahead. George wants to rest, to hold back a moment, but he's scared that if he does, he'll be left alone. He wants to call out, wants to say, *Stop, wait*, wants to say, *Let's not look, this is enough, let's go back*, but he can barely breathe, let alone shout.

He gulps at the air and tries to stand upright against the slope, swaying, trying to keep his balance.

"Julia!"

It comes out as a raspy, broken thing, snatched away by the wind almost before it leaves his mouth, but it's enough.

She stops.

She is waiting for him, and George lets out a breath that is almost a sob, scrambling up faster to join her. Even as he closes the distance, he knows something is wrong. She is too still, her back too straight. She's not looking back at him. He reaches her and realizes why.

They've reached the top.

George isn't sure how long they stand together looking down into the valley. He only knows that it ends when Julia reaches over and takes his hand to pull him away. She does it very gently and he lets himself be led. He thinks he might fall without her. His limbs feel clumsy and mechanical. No one has held his hand like this, to guide his way, in a long time, not for years. She must have done this for Tom once, when they were both much younger.

When the ground levels out, just before the tree line, he lets go to wipe at his wet face. Julia turns her head away, giving him privacy.

For a moment he presses his hands into his face very tightly, counting breaths. When he closes his eyes, he can see it again, all tangled up in the telephone wires in that horrible scraped out wound in the earth, dripping out a dark stain. He keeps his eyes open, looks at the pink light between his fingers instead.

Julia says something, but it's lost in the wind and George takes his hands away from his eyes to look at her. The yellow hood has fallen down. A strand of hair is stuck to the corner of Julia's mouth, but she doesn't brush it away. She doesn't even seem to notice.

"What?" George asks. "What did you say?"

"It couldn't have survived," Julia says and the way she says it sounds like a question.

"It was dead," George says and when she looks at him, he says it again, to make sure she knows he means it. "It was dead."

They reach the trees and keep moving.

They walk side by side now, keeping close even though it makes the path more difficult to navigate. Julia holds back a branch to let him through and George glances at her face as he passes through the gap. He looks for some sign in her face, some lasting mark to reflect back at him the truth of what they've seen. She should look older, but she doesn't look any different than this morning. Her mouth is a thin, hard line, lips pressed so tightly together that it seems impossible that she could ever speak again.

Even so, George wants to ask her. He wants to ask her if she will be okay. He wants to ask her if it made a difference, coming out here today, if it was better to know, to see it for themselves.

"It's getting dark," he says.

"I know. But it's not far now."

He wants to ask, how could it be that big, how could it be possible for something like that to exist in the same world as his bike and their village? He wants to ask about the telephone wires and if she remembers the stories she used to make up or if he imagined that, if maybe he imagined a life before this, a life that was normal and safe and small.

He wants to ask her what happened after he walked the plank, after the sharks and the raft. He wants to ask her how it all ended.

Maybe she'll smile at him and laugh and say, *I remember. I remember that story. It never stopped. It just kept going.*

For now though, with the shadows gathering, they keep walking, as above them small snowflakes escape the net of dark branches and fall softly, soundlessly, to the ground.

See Maud Woolf's story "The Stranding" online at Metaphorosis.
If you liked it, leave a comment. Authors love that!
Remember to subscribe to our e-mail updates so you'll know when new stories are posted.

About the story

I grew up in a small Scottish coastal village, much like the one in "The Stranding". While it was a bustling tourist spot in summer, in winter the place became bleak and abandoned. The only bus to town came infrequently and my friends and I spent most of our time rambling around by the beach and in the fields nearby. Driven by boredom we went swimming in large rockpools and tried, mostly without success, to light small fires from the driftwood. Once, we crawled on our bellies through the large storm drain that ran under the town, but this experience was frightening and never repeated.

Living near the beach you see a lot of things washed up with the tide. Most of these things were already dead, but one September twenty-seven live pilot whales beached themselves on the rocky coast that ran between our village and the next. My friend and I took a bus to see them, talking so much we became breathless and bouncing in our seats in anticipation. We had never seen a live whale before, not even as distant lumps between the waves. We weren't the only ones excited; the bus was crowded and most of us got off at the same stop. Not much happened in the countryside and this felt like an event. I won't say too much about what we saw, only that of the twenty-seven whales stranded, only ten made it back to the water. The bus ride home was silent.

Although it affected me at the time, I filed this memory away and had almost forgotten about it completely until quite recently. During the first UK lockdown, I was living in Bristol and spent most of my time taking long, solitary walks. I remember thinking how strange it was to see nothing but empty streets but also how strangely familiar the experience was. An idea started creeping in, or, to be more accurate, an image. Two kids walking through a silent village in the snow. Setting out to find something.

Details like what it was they were hoping to find and why the streets were empty came later, but that initial image is still crystal clear in my head, even now. I couldn't write about the whales, and I didn't want to write about the pandemic. I wrote "The Stranding" instead and that, I think, was a pretty good alternative to both.

A question for the author

Q: What would your animal totem be?

A: I don't know if I would call them an animal totem, but I've always felt a strong affinity with magpies. I remember my grandmother teaching me to use them as omens (one for sorrow, two for joy) and even now, when I see them, I start counting. They may be known as thieves, but to me to me the act of writing often feels like thievery. Shiny objects are like good stories, to be looked out for and hoarded jealously.

About the author

Maud Woolf is Scottish writer with a particular interest in speculative fiction. Currently working towards an MLitt in Creative Writing at the University of Glasgow, most of her free time is spent either writing in the library or searching for a way into the city's abandoned network of underground tunnels.

@WoolfWolf

The Nocturnals II

Mariah Montoya

In a world where each day and night lasts thirty years, Joah Cadshaw is searching for a missing boy. Before he can find him, bells start ringing throughout the streets; it's time for his community to migrate east, toward the fading daylight, before the decades-long darkness and its night monsters overtake them all. Joah and his new partner, Misla Crane, embark on a quest out west to warn the people who don't know it's time to Move.

On their journey, Joah finds evidence that the missing boy may have been abducted by the Nocturnals—the feared humanoid creatures of the Eternal Night. Joah vows to bring him home.

Part 2

"Hey, Hicks, get up. Retrievers are here."

Hickory Glade groaned in his bundle of blankets, thumbing his pounding temples. His tent-mate had poked his head through the open flap to wake him, but the ice moon was still hovering above the northern skyline, sending a stripe of brilliant white through the canvas.

"Retrievers?" Hickory said, sitting up. "What the hell d'you mean, retrievers?"

Scowling, he checked the timepiece strapped to his wrist. Unlike the rest of the Sunsetters, who started Moving when the sun hung ten degrees above the horizon, the miners didn't have to pack up until five: at five degrees, the sun dangled low in the sky and nighttime prowled just around the corner.

But the hand of Hickory's watch still hovered over the spindly number seven. Not quite late enough to start chasing daylight like they had to do every two damn years. *Strange.* Retrievers usually only showed up when someone—some hunter or scavenger or miner—had gotten lost out in the woods and needed their asses saved from the Eternal Night.

"Yeah, retrievers," Sid said, pushing aside the flap so that smoke and murmurs filled the tent. "Apparently they've got something to tell us. General D's orders. C'mon."

Hickory groaned, stretched, and cracked his neck with a swift jerk of his head. Something felt off, as if warning bells were clanging in the back of his mind. Loud voices and crude jokes usually speared the morning air, but now he only heard gruff whispers and rumbles, quiet, anxious words masked by the roar of the distant river that ran along the edge of their campground.

"Alright, alright, I'm getting up. Wait for me, asshole."

He shook away his blankets and pushed through the dew-slick flap, following Sid to the wooded area outside their caverns. Here, a crowd of soot-faced miners elbowed each other and craned their necks to look at whoever stood in the center of the clearing.

Hickory wasted no time, shoving past his comrades until he had squeezed his way to the front of the pack. He jerked to a gut-wrenching stop when he saw who the two retrievers were.

No, it couldn't be.

Joah Cadshaw. *Joah Cadshaw* was poised in front of the conglomeration of tents and ashy, smoking firepit, his hands clasped neatly behind his back. Hickory rubbed his eyes, but when he opened them again, the horrible apparition was still there. Cadshaw was dressed in a tight, plain white shirt, very different from the crisp retriever uniform he'd used to wear. His hair was ruffled, his chin stubbled, his frame skinnier than the last time Hickory had seen him.

And he, Joah Fucking Cadshaw, was standing elbow to elbow with—

"*Misla*," Hickory spat, cutting through the low grumble of conversation.

When he said her name, the branches around them seemed to still, and the beetles scuttling up their trunks seemed to slow. The distant river, however, thundered with the spite thudding through Hickory's veins. Angry, white foam filled his chest.

"What the hell are you doing here? With *him*?"

The miners coughed themselves into awkward silence. Joah Cadshaw spotted him with the faintest spike of surprise, eyebrows lifting a fraction and narrowing again.

Misla Crane couldn't stifle *her* shock, though. Tilting her head, she said, "Hickory?" in that sickeningly sweet voice she had always used around him, the innocent one. It made him want to throw her onto a bed and pound that silly innocence out of her.

"You two know each other?" Cadshaw asked coldly.

"Yes, you Nocturnal-loving freak, Misla and I *know* each other." Hickory lurched forward, but rough hands cupped his shoulders, holding him back. "She was my girl. She was *mine*, and now you've taken her, just like you took everything else from me. Let me *go*."

But Sid's hold only tightened, and Hickory's worst memory swirled before him:

It was thirteen degrees. He stood in the middle of the High Road before the executioner's block, his ax glinting in the sun. People lined the road in thick rivers of hot bodies and excited whispers, watching as the retriever in the distance led his prisoner toward them. An Infected's execution was usually an exciting ordeal, but this time it was even more so: it was the retriever's own wife *who had been infected, the retriever's own* wife *Hickory would kill.*

He licked his lips, tasting the salt of his own sweet sweat. He'd never liked Joah Cadshaw. Ignorant, cocky prick. If he could pull the man's guts through his neck and dangle them around his own, he'd wear the necklace every damn arcsec. It served him right, in a way, that the Nocturnals had chosen to infect Blair Cadshaw. They picked one victim a year to lure to their shit-pit of never-ending darkness; Retriever Cadshaw had always tracked these victims down with ease, forcing them back to their deaths before they could sneak back on their own and wreak havoc on the community. Hickory himself had never hid his fascination with his ax, but Cadshaw had always pretended to be repulsed by the whole ordeal. A reluctant hero.

Until now.

Now Hickory could see, as Cadshaw and his chained wife drew nearer: the famous retriever was actually *repulsed. Pain twisted his face. When he finally reached the executioner's block, he*

addressed   the   man   sitting   behind
Hickory's post, desperation in his voice.

"I beg you to reconsider, General. I think
she's trying to tell us something."

At his words, the woman opened her
mouth and screamed, "WARN. WARN.
WARN." Drool swung from her teeth. She
looked as insane as all the other Infected
scum Hickory had gotten rid of before, but
behind him, General Deckler made a grunt
of pity.

"I can postpone the execution if you
have   sufficient   proof   that   she   is   not
dangerous."

"What?" Hickory spat, spinning around.

The general had always loved Joah
Cadshaw, true, but why was he falling for
such a biased pile of shit? Even as Hickory
watched, the Infected woman swiped a
pale, clammy hand toward the onlookers,
that drool soaking through her shirt.

No, she was still dangerous. Cadshaw
would put them all at risk because he
would never quit loving the monster his
wife had become.

"I'll consider a life extension," General
Deckler   began,   but   Hickory   marched
forward. Before Cadshaw could blink,
before the crowd could gasp, he raised his
weapon. The blade sliced cleanly through

the Infected woman's neck. Her head hit the ground with a thud.

A shivering silence.

Then Cadshaw was screaming. He threw himself forward and tried to wrestle the ax from Hickory's hand. His eyes bulged, and Hickory clung to his ax like a lifeline, and they threw each other to the High Road, rolling in Blair's blood, the blade narrowly missing Hickory's left ear...

General Deckler's men had jumped in to break them apart. Afterward, Hickory had been fired for misconduct, but Cadshaw himself had simply been transferred to another department for his own "mental wellbeing," or some soft-hearted, bullshit excuse like that. Hickory had watched in a drunken stupor as Misla, once an angelic little creature he'd wooed and won with all the right words, had packed her things and left him. He'd become like a headless pheasant, staggering around, making a wage by pounding grahsm from cave interiors like his father had once done. A regression in familial stance for sure.

"You lost me my job!" he said now, jerking against the arms wrapped around him. It wasn't fair that he, Hickory, was still out *here*, while Cadshaw had obviously wormed his way back into a retrieving position. Always General D's favorite, that was for bloody sure.

"Well, you killed my wife, so consider us even."

Cadshaw wasn't trembling, but his face had turned a blotchy, veiny purple that made Hickory feel triumphant. Oh, the mask was there, but it was slipping.

"Well, it looks like you paid me back, didn't you?" Hickory panted. "Looks like you've gone and stolen *my* woman. Is that why you left then, pretty girl? So you could be with *him*?"

He bit his lip. Tasted blood. His last encounter with Misla had not been pleasant, he had to admit, but she didn't look the worse for wear. She was wearing the same fitted white shirt Cadshaw was, but hers hugged her curves, and she had added a frayed scarf that bore a resemblance to the Retrieving Institute colors. She was plumper than he'd last seen her. Her hips were wider, her breasts lower, her cheeks rounder. A good weight gain. It added a flush to her face, a look of strength in her thighs.

But her eyes weren't flickering downward like they'd used to. They squinted at him with no trace of that soft, liquidy warmth he had come to associate with melting candle wax. These new eyes looked hard and gray and unyielding.

Before Hickory could say anything else, Misla cupped her hands around her mouth to address the crowd, as if his outburst had been nothing more than the irritating chirp of crickets.

"The Moving bells rang early because the High Road was severed."

At that word, *severed*, Hickory saw Blair Cadshaw's head at his shoes. The wisps of her hair brushing his ankles. Her blood soaking into the asphalt of the High Road.

"We have to stray from the road our ancestors have been using for centuries," Misla continued. "You all need to pack up immediately." She paused, glanced at Hickory, and cleared her throat, throwing a braid over her shoulder. "It's been easy to follow the sun our whole lives, because we can travel four times as fast. But this detour will slow us down. The Nocturnals won't be far behind."

"Any questions?" Cadshaw asked, his eyes trained on Hickory.

"Well, how come the High Road was severed?" someone called.

"We don't know," Misla said. "Possibly a quake. Some kind of natural disaster. Either way, it's going to take longer than expected to reach the Green Sea. So get Moving."

With that, *Hickory's* woman—yes, she was still Hickory's woman, he felt that deep within him—whipped around with her new bravado and strode back through the path of trees, that frayed scarf bouncing on her neck, Joah Cadshaw on her heel.

The arms holding him back loosened. Hickory turned to see Sid raise an eyebrow at him as the rest of the miners burst into movement, tearing down tents and lugging supplies to the pack horses in another clearing through the trees.

"Sorry, Hicks, had to do it," Sid said. "Couldn't let you kill the nut. Though I guess if you had, there's no General Deckler around to fire you."

"Good Old General D's *obsessed* with Joah." Hickory licked the last beads of blood from the cracks in his lips. "I knew it back then—if Joah wanted to delay his wife's execution, Deckler wouldn't just grant the wish. He'd blow kisses into Joah's asshole too, for good measure." Hickory mimed a kiss without humor. "If I killed him now, the general would track me down and staple my face to his office wall, right next to that shiny Nocturnal poster of his."

Apparently, Sid decided this was funny, because he belly-chuckled. The tension cracked inside Hickory, who laughed with him, eyes tracking the last patches of Misla's new, widened ass as she pushed through branches and disappeared in the thickness of the trees.

"So," Sid continued when they had quit laughing. He spit into the nearest fire. A coal sizzled. "You ready to Move, Hicks? The city's so slow, we'll catch up to those slugs in no time. Might as well bring the shiniest grahsm with us. Get some extra silvers for it."

"Oh, I'm ready to Move," Hickory said, still gazing at the place where Misla had melted into the woods. He could practically feel her shrill breath in his ears again, but that may have been the sudden breeze whistling between the trees. "I'm not Moving toward the sun, though."

Sid's eyebrows reached his shiny, slick hairline. Hickory laughed.

"I can't let him steal her again. I'm going to get my girl back." He paused, imagining Aoif Deckler. "I think my face getting stapled to a wall is a risk I'm willing to take."

Joah and Misla left seven degrees behind them like an old, fallen-off shoe.

When they reached six degrees a dozen arcsecs later, the sun cast dark purple shadows; its rays had shrunk until it resembled a neat orange ball hovering inches from the horizon behind them.

"Oil scavengers should've started Moving by now," Joah told Misla, forcing himself to sound as if he hadn't just exchanged words with his wife's killer. "We'll probably pass them on the High Road. We've just got to make it to that tower near the oil reserves, make sure no one got left behind. Then we can head back."

"Right," Misla said.

Five degrees. They continued in dense silence. The stretch of forest and caves where the miners had been residing morphed back into tall, naked cliffs, as if they were entering a dead zone between two forests. Beyond the tower, Joah knew, the woods would rejuvenate.

Four degrees. They'd be passing the scavengers any moment, but Joah hardly cared. His whole being quivered with suppressed rage. Oh, why hadn't he just charged at the man? Why hadn't he finally killed the monster haunting his dreams? And why hadn't Misla mentioned it—that she'd dated such a beast? That *he* was the one who had burned and abused her?

I was there when it happened, you know, she had told him. *In the crowd...*

Three degrees. Dark shadows leapt across the High Road. *Hares*, Joah thought numbly.

Then the steed's magnetic clock read two degrees, the bright blue of the sky glistened with dark streaks of orange, and he couldn't restrain his words anymore.

"It was him—" he began.

He glanced at her. His breath caught on his tongue. Under different circumstances, the new lighting might have made her beautiful. But dried tears striped her cheeks, and those smile-shaped scratches marked the hollows of her neck, which she had tried to hide by wrapping the tattered remains of her retrieving uniform around her throat like a scarf.

"It was Hickory Glade?" he grunted, before he could swallow himself into more silence. "You dated him? He's the one who gave you your scar?" *And mine*, he didn't add.

Misla sighed.

"He was charming, at first. He always told me the most fantastic *stories*. Some were about his father. The miner. He told me all about his dad's adventures, how his dad had discovered magic metals and secret caves, how he would come home with beautiful stones for their rock collection. Hickory still had those stones. He kept them in empty jars and placed them all around his house, and in the darkness lit by fire, it was all so...so *beautiful*."

Joah knew for a fact that Hickory Glade had loathed his status as a simple miner's son, had only told these stories to glorify the poverty-stricken childhood he had grown up in.

"But most," Misla continued, and her next words came as no surprise, "were about his grandfather. The general before Deckler. He told me about his grandfather's rise to leadership. How he developed the warning system. How he died. Hickory talked a lot about how he died."

Joah knew that Hickory's grandfather had been killed by Nocturnals about six decades ago. But he couldn't force himself to conjure any pity. He stared ahead as the High Road made a sharp bend around a crag. With the light dimming, branches and twigs that jutted from the cliffs looked more and more like long, crooked fingers. There were occasional muffled hoots and far-off yowls that sounded like glitches in the normal noise of life.

"Listen, Joah," Misla said earnestly. "I left Hickory after he murdered your wife."

Murdered.

Chills wormed up Joah's spine at that word. Not killed. Not executed. *Murdered.*

He stared without seeing at the bluffs before them. Everyone else had considered his wife's death a violation of procedure. Hickory Glade had been fired for misconduct, not *murder.*

Yet, finally, here was someone who believed otherwise like him.

"I always suspected Hickory enjoyed his little executions," Misla continued in a deadpan voice. "He always convinced me otherwise. He told me it was for the good of the Sunsetters. He was saving children's lives. The Nocturnals and everyone they infected were demons that would infest our community if left untreated. It wasn't until he swung that ax before General Deckler's say-so that I knew he'd been lying. He *liked* killing. I could see it on his face when—well..."

"Yeah," Joah managed to choke out.

The crests of the distant mountains glowed purple, like the treetops had caught a violet fire. Migrating birds freckled the sky. At the thought of birds, Joah became distinctly aware of the cushioning in his back pocket: the remains of young Damien Fertheli's green cat shirt. Evidence that the Nocturnals had gotten into the head of a child.

Misla had asked about the shirt after they had scrambled into their sleeping bags three cycles ago, but he hadn't found the right words, had instead mumbled something about making sure she finish cleaning and wrapping her cuts. Now, though, after seeing the way she had addressed the miners so calmly in the face of her fanatic ex, he knew he had to tell her about the Infected boy.

He opened his mouth, but Misla spoke before he could.

"Anyway, I decided to become a retriever after I left Hickory. I've always hated how we behead the Infected as *soon* as we bring them back—"

"Not true," Joah retorted. The green shirt was pushed momentarily from his mind. "If we can drag them back before they reach... well, what you'd call the Eternal Night, we put them in a white room and wait to see if the madness subsides. Sometimes it does. More often it doesn't. But the public doesn't see that. The public only sees the Infected that managed to make physical contact with the Nocturnals, the ones who sneak back after a few years to ravage our community. Retrievers track down *those* ones before they can surprise-ambush us —"

"I know, Boss," Misla cut in. "I just graduated from the Retrieving Institute. I got top marks, you know. All that you just said was in our senior exam."

"Well, what's your *point*, Crane?"

"I want," said Misla, with a breath so deep it seemed to suck the air from Joah's own lungs, "to see if the Infected can talk to the Nocturnals and find out what they want."

Joah's heart thrashed against his ribs. All thoughts of telling Misla about the ripped green shirt in his pocket fluttered away, alongside the migrating birds overhead.

"Crane..." He tried to sound casual. "You don't think I tried talking to every single Infected person I brought back? You don't think I delayed missions to interrogate them?"

She looked at him. He kept his eyes pasted on the winding High Road. Fat rodents were pattering across their path now. He swerved to avoid running them over.

"You don't think I purposely ran out of fuel to give the Infected extra time to heal? You don't think I spent a whole *year* with my crazed wife out here in the wilderness trying to find a cure, only to fail, only for General Deckler to send more retrievers to force us back with a death penalty hanging over my head as well as hers?"

"I didn't—"

"Of course you didn't know." Snot clogged Joah's throat. "Everyone thinks retrievers are cold and cruel. But once the Nocturnals lodge their whispers into your head, they don't withdraw those whispers

—but, of course, you'd already know that. Retrieving Institute, and all, right?"

"Look," Misla said, crossing her arms, "I know you're bitter. I know you're sad. But you don't need to treat me like—like—*scavengers.*"

"Like scavengers?" Joah repeated.

"No. Look. Scavengers."

Misla pointed through their cracked windshield. During their conversation, the High Road had rounded a cliff and continued into a wide expanse of hardened, rocky aro. Now, perched on the opening beyond, the outline of a cylindrical tower bowed over the High Road.

But the High Road wasn't empty. Each strapped with bouncing silver canteens, sprinting toward them, were the oil scavengers who should have started Moving five degrees before. They were hollering indistinguishably, their voices like blunt knives failing to slice the air.

Cursing, Joah sped toward them until they were close enough to hear each gasping word.

"Hey, hey, hey!"

"Did General Deckler send you?"

"Thank God you're here."

Joah punched the brakes as they met the scavengers, who were coughing and panting. Their mops of hair were gray with dust. Their hands were slimy with oil and blood.

"Hold up." Joah tugged on the parking stick and jumped out onto the dusted High Road to meet them. "It's almost sunset. Why the *hell* are you lot still here? I thought you might've taken a shortcut and that's why we didn't see you on the High Road, but I never thought—"

"Mack got killed," one scavenger piped up, breathless. "He's my friend, Mack is. *Was*, I mean. A night beast came braver than usual. Tiptoed into sunset. It got Mack—"

"And all our damn horses," another scavenger added.

"Aye, and all our horses," the first scavenger agreed, "it's like nothing I've never seen in my life. Like a cat, but bigger, and it's got scales."

"The night beast is some kind of reptile, you mean?" Misla asked.

All the men's eyes flashed over to her, as if they had permission now that she had spoken. They scanned her body for much too long, some with smirks.

"I guess," said the scavenger, his eyes on Misla's chest, "but a cat-like reptile."

"And how did this creature kill your friend?"

"It yowled at 'im. Horrible yowl, could've burst your eardrums. And Mack dropped to the ground, screaming and twitching. And then the cat drug him away into the forest by its claws. Same with the horses."

Joah and Misla exchanged glances. A grim understanding shot between them.

"You're sure it was a night beast?" Joah asked.

"Aye. Stayed in the shadows the whole time. Not that that's too hard, with the forest a little way back, and the tower. That tower makes a *long* shadow."

The group all turned to gaze at the strange construction, which looked, Joah thought, like a giant canine tooth, fat and round at the bottom, tapered and sharp on top. It was far larger and more permanent than anything the Sunsetters had ever created in living history. It had been quite the object of horror stories and conspiracy theories as they had passed it during the last Move, but General Deckler had been firm about Moving by, not staying to investigate. Only after they had settled had he sent some men back to collect the oil in a nearby reservoir.

"Can we ride back with you?" the first scavenger asked now. His canteen was dripping beads of that oil onto the dirt of the High Road. "We could cram in the back if we threw some stuff out." He peered through the window. "You don't need them tents if we head back now, and we'd only need 'bout half those cans if we ration. Should make it back in three cycles, yeah?"

Joah and Misla passed that knowing look again. Dimly, Joah felt warm surprise that they could already communicate the vague basics without speaking.

"You won't make it back before three moon cycles," Misla said firmly. "And Retriever Cadshaw and I aren't going back just yet, so no, you can't hitch a ride with us."

"Come again?" the scavenger asked.

"The Sunsetters already Moved." Briefly, Joah explained the fissure in the High Road. "Retriever Crane and I are going to investigate the creature that killed your friend. If the night beasts are starting to chance sunlight, General Deckler needs to know about it."

And we need to search for the boy, he didn't add.

"We'll give you some of our food," Misla said. "If you stick together and keep a steady pace, you should be fine. Just veer right after the grasslands. You might even catch up to the grahsm miners, they just left and there are a lot more of them, so they'll be slower than—"

Joah saw it coming a second before it happened.

The first scavenger tilted his head, his eyes flickering toward his mates, his pupils gleaming with that dog-like hunger for survival. His lip curled upward. His mates gave wisps of laughter, like schoolgirls giggling behind polite hands when a boy is doomed for detention.

"Crane, DOWN," Joah bellowed.

Misla didn't hesitate. She thudded to her knees; the scavenger's swinging fist missed her head by an inch, but another one, shiny with oil and dirt, met Joah's ear.

His skull exploded. His lungs seemed to jump out of his throat. Boots connected with his body from every direction. The High Road pounded his spine again and again, like a crazed, violent mother burping her baby. Dust heated his throat.

Far off, Joah thought Misla might be climbing the shafts of orange light in the sky like a stairwell, screaming his name. *Strange.* He couldn't remember who Misla was, exactly, but he thought perhaps she was his wife. Perhaps she was beautiful.

Then the scavengers gave his ribs a final kick, and the Eternal Night folded him in its calm, cold embrace.

Sleep cocooned him. No light disturbed his darkness and no sound punctuated his silence. It was as if he lay in a black pond, where the waves lapped over him seamlessly, lulling him into a cavern where light and sound didn't exist. And there was no light and there was no sound. No light or sound. Light or sound. Light. Sound.

A dull pounding sensation hammered the back of his head. It was not light *or* sound, but a *feeling*, like a beam of bright noise thumping itself into his skull.

"Stop it," Joah muttered, swiping his hand at the beam.

"Joah," the beam said back.

His eyelids betrayed him, opening him up to a bright, noisy world. A woman was leaning over him, chanting his name over and over, the left side of her face blotched and purple. The ice moon beamed beyond her shoulders.

"Keep waking up, Joah," the woman said, and her name came to him.

"Misla." He tried to sit up. The world tilted. The waves came back and spiraled around him. The woman pressed a palm to his chest and forced him to lie back down.

"Hey, hey, not so fast, take it slow, you'll be alright, just take it slow."

She said this all very fast, and her urgency cut through Joah's haze in a way the moon's ferocity couldn't. He blinked. He gazed at the bruise masking her left eye and cursed.

"They hit you," he mumbled. "The scavengers. Scum. Vultures. They hit you."

"They did a lot worse to you," Misla said. "I only wish I could've broken all their bones before they ran off. But I— there were too many of them. I think I knocked out a tooth, but…"

Her eyes darted left and right. For the first time, Joah became aware of how bright the moon was, stamped against the blackening purple sky. He tilted his head to find the sun, but it had shrunk to half a dome peeking between two cliffs behind them—a bloodred eye peering at them cruelly. Preparing to blink into nothingness.

"They took the steed, didn't they?" Joah spat, using his elbows to prop himself up.

Every inch of him ached. He did a quick self-evaluation and guessed he was concussed, with bruised ribs and a broken nose. Dried blood caked his upper lip. His jaw throbbed.

"Yes, they took the steed. Didn't leave us any food, either. They told me to kiss the sun's fiery red ass goodbye."

"How thoughtful," Joah growled.

"I know, right? Now, first things first, we need to get out of the open. If there really *are* night beasts lurking around, I'd rather not meet them for the first time with a damaged partner."

She paused, those eyes darting again. The noise of sunset swelled, but Joah couldn't tell where the creatures were, exactly; it sounded as if all the chirps and coos and cries were simply eddying around his head, ringing in his ears. As if the rocks were shrieking.

"I say we get to that tower," he grunted, nodding toward them. "I don't know if you got a good look when we passed by during the last Move. *I* didn't see any doors, but looks like it's made of metal. It'll retain the sun's heat long enough for us to form some kind of plan." He huffed as he tried to stand. "After the sun sets, it can get cold. Fast."

"Okay, tower it is. But don't crap yourself trying to get up so fast. Let me help."

Misla placed her hands in Joah's armpits and hoisted him up. He bit his lip to keep himself from crying out, then gasped anyway as his teeth pierced an already mangled lip.

"Don't worry, you can make as much noise as you'd like. I won't laugh."

"You're too kind."

Misla's lips twitched as they hobbled toward the outline of the tower before them, Joah's arm hooked around her neck, the moon glowing brighter above them. Sometimes he glanced sideways and mashed his teeth together at the sight of the bruise that had spread from her eyebrow to cheekbone. When—*if*—they caught up to the rest of the community, he'd have Deckler throw the scavengers in the smelliest portable prisons, *that* was for sure.

Greasy, slimy sons of Dirt Slum bitches, he thought. *Cowardly piles of shit...*

But as the tower rose, grating the gray mob of clouds that had accumulated in the sky, Joah's internal curses gave way to a dizziness. His fingertips tingled. Even as Aoif Deckler's best retriever, he had only ever ventured this far into the darkness once before...

He was standing in a meadow. Clouds fragmented the sky, casting a bloody light on the stretch of never-ending grasses and tufts of violet wildflowers. A figure was swaying in the distance, walking away from him, chanting something indiscernible as she staggered westward.

"Almost there," Misla muttered. "Come on, just a little further."

Joah stared at the figure, knowing it was her. Her, her, her. The one he'd been chasing for a year now, the one who, the night before she'd run away, had whispered against his neck that she wanted to try for a baby soon.

"Joah, I—I think there *is* a door. Or some kind of opening. Look."

He tried to look, but *she had wanted to be a mother. Now she would never be a* mother. She was a Nocturnal puppet, and Joah was almost too scared to call out her name. But he did call out her name, and despite what they said about the Infected's inability to understand language after the Nocturnals had twined words around their brains, she turned.

She turned.

She turned, and Joah saw the face of his wife wearing a mask of purest white. Bright purple veins crisscrossed her cheeks and forehead, like shattered eggshells.

No, it was not his wife's face, but the ice moon posing as his wife's face. He felt a newfound tickle, like a stroking finger, caress the back of his neck. A dim part of him realized that the moon was king. Maybe not king of the day, but king of the Eternal Night. And now it had plastered itself over his wife's eyes, and it was laughing at him.

Her manic smile spread her cheeks as she hobbled toward him, arms outstretched...

"Stay with me, Joah, don't fall asleep yet."

Hazily, Joah saw Misla push through a blanket of wool-like cobwebs and help him through a rounded hole in steel, into a cavern of deepest pitch-black. Their shoes crunched over brittle objects scattered on the floor. Misla was saying something else to him, but he couldn't hear. Tingles scuttled up his spine, as if his wife were *in his arms now. She was laughing up at him. Her eyes twitched in their sockets, like a rat was squirming beneath her eyelids, desperate to break free and nibble at Joah's skin.*

Blair, *he cried.* Blair, Blair, Blair.

But she just laughed and laughed and squeaked, "Warn you. Got to," *and then kept laughing, her tongue shooting in and out, her mouth so widely stretched he could see her uvula and each rotten tooth, and he knew then, although he would try to find her a cure later, that she was gone. Her body was here, but the Nocturnals had snatched her soul right out of his cradling arms. She was gone.*

"Gone," Joah croaked. "Gone. All gone."

"What are you talking about, Joah? I'm right here. Just lean back. One moment."

Misla's warmth disappeared. He was alone, his back pressed against a smooth, cold surface. His head throbbed. When he pressed his hands against the floor to steady himself, something sharp pierced his right palm. He sucked in a breath that made his chest ache.

"Come back, Misla," he murmured.

She didn't answer. He blinked, trying to rid himself of the memories infecting him so that he could assess his present situation.

He was slumped against the wall of what felt like a smooth cave. But the mouth, through which streamed a glum pool of bruised purple light, was perfectly square, and there had been no caves surrounding the High Road. He had told Misla to take him to the tower.

Somehow, then, she had lugged him *inside* the structure. As his eyes adjusted to the darkness, Joah saw that there was a hole in the floor, like a giant toilet bowl that might flush away anything wandering in its path. And surrounding the hole in a swirl...

Bones. Tiny skulls. Bird beaks. The skeletons of hares, rats, and other animals Joah knew no name for.

"Misla!" he called, louder, his eyes racing toward that inexplicable entrance.

She appeared at the door, illuminated by a ball of fire. He stared, dazed, as she hurried inside, bringing the fire with her. That flickering kind of light was usually only used for cooking, but Hickory Glade must have taught her how to make torches, because Misla had wrapped the remaining slice of her retriever's uniform around a dead branch.

"Glad to see you're awake," she said, closing the door behind her. The bruised purple light gave way to dancing flames as she skirted carefully around the hole leading underground.

"Yeah, glad to be awake," Joah mumbled.

They gazed around them, Misla's firelight illuminating their surroundings. Near the closed door, a stone staircase wrapped around the edge of the tower until it disappeared through the floor above. But Joah could not stop staring at the staircase that began at the edge of the hole in the ground and spiraled downward, into whatever abyss had been created beneath the tower.

"We'll—we'll be safe in here, I think." Misla started toward him, picking her way carefully so as to avoid stepping on skulls. "The night beasts can't get to us if—"

"But Misla, how did these *bones* get in here?" It took every ounce of determination to speak coherently. "I doubt all the sunset critters decided to have a death party inside a man-made building." Joah paused, his head spinning. "I...I just don't like this, Misla. Where'd that door *come* from? We—I—nobody saw any openings when we passed by during the Move."

"Maybe we all missed it." Misla bent down beside him. One hand still gripping the torch, she dug into her pocket and brought out a familiar green capsule. "Here, take this. It's the pain medication you wanted me to use after those birds attacked me."

"You didn't take—?"

"Oh, don't give me that look. It ended up working out. You need relief more than I did."

Joah grumbled, but swallowed the pill dry, realizing as he did so how his throat burned with a parched aridness. The scavengers hadn't even left them a water canteen, for God's sake. He opened his mouth to ask if Misla knew of any new curse words he could use, but she rammed a finger to her lips, nodding toward the ceiling.

A strange screeching noise, like grinding metal gears, echoed above them. Then came a *thump*, and a *clang*, as if something were banging two kitchen pans against each other.

Slowly, Misla bent and picked up a sharp, curved bone, holding it in a tight fist like a dagger. Her torch's fire danced and waved eagerly, its flames reaching toward the ceiling. Toward whatever night beast they had trapped themselves in this God-forsaken tower with.

Maybe it was the same reptilian beast that had hoarded all these skeletons, Joah thought with a barely suppressed moan. The same beast that had killed the scavenger Mack.

"Misla, what are you doing?" he hissed suddenly.

She had turned to creep toward the staircase by the door, torch in one hand, bone in the other. When Joah made to stand, she whispered, "I'm going to check it out. You stay there. You won't be able to help in your condition, so find yourself a sharp one and stay awake."

"Misla, *no*."

But she was already climbing those stairs, which were steeper than the portable ones leading up to Aoif Deckler's office. They had no side railings, and Misla kept her shoulder pressed against the tower wall as she stole upward, around and around, until she had ascended to the landing above. Her absence brought a horrible, mud-thick darkness.

"Shit. Shit. Shit." Joah pressed his shoulder blades against the wall to scoot himself up. His body ached, but the sharp, dizzying agony he had expected did not come. The capsules worked fast, then, or else his panic had overpowered the pain.

Please be a hare, or a possum, or any kind of small, harmless creature, Joah pleaded as he limped his way around the hole and toward the staircase, hands outstretched in the darkness. But even as he lugged his foot onto the first stone step, he heard a shrill, keening wail above him.

"I'm coming, Misla, I'm coming!"

Now he was bounding up the steps, ignoring his body's aching protests. The staircase rose until it met a rounded opening in the ceiling, and then Joah was panting in a perfectly circular room lit with Misla's torch like the one below. Except there were no skeletons infesting this one's floor. Instead, spirals of steel hung from the ceiling, and Misla was crouching before—not a night beast—but a boy.

"Damien," Joah whispered, awe-struck.

The boy was naked, but so muddy it looked as if he had developed a new, thick layer of armor. Even so, Joah recognized his face as the same one plastered on sketches in his office. He also recognized the Infected wildness that had crept into the boy's eyes, the look of shattered eggshells and popping purple veins and a moon-like glow shrouding his features.

"You know him?" Misla demanded.

She had dropped her weapon, which lay discarded at the boy's feet. Damien was shuffling and panting. He seemed unsure of where he was. There was no hint of that wry smile that Blair had given, only a delirious confusion, the cries of a small babe calling for his mother.

"I—he's—his name's Damien Fertheli. He's—" Dazed, Joah reached into his pocket and brought out the limp scrap of green shirt he had plucked from the High Road. He held it out to the boy, then shook his head. "What the hell am I doing? Here, Damien."

He pulled off his own shirt. Tentatively, trying to keep steady, he slipped it over the boy's head. Damien only jerked away half-heartedly. A good sign. Joah grabbed the boy's hands—which were cold as the dead of night—and forced them through the sleeves.

The bottom hem unraveled to Damien's knees, so that, in the firelight, it looked as if the Infected child had donned a translucent, moon-woven dress.

Misla inhaled, but she wasn't staring at the boy. She switched the torch to her other hand and squinted at Joah's midriff. Damien let out another wail.

Joah looked down. His body glowed blue and green with bruises. They covered his ribs and chest like ripples in a pool. And suddenly it seemed as if the three of them, standing together, formed an eerie, indoor sunset: Misla, with her dwindling blaze of orange like the dying sun; Damien, in his egg-white dress like the ice moon; and Joah, the bruises painted over his body like the looming darkness that came with the Eternal Night.

Then Misla retracted her firelight. The spell was broken.

"How," she asked in a wavering voice, "do you know this boy? *How is he here?*"

Joah's legs couldn't hold him anymore; the pain had crept back into his head and lungs and ribs. He lowered himself to the floor as Damien wailed again.

"Do you remember when we first met? How Deckler told me to 'forget the boy'?"

Misla nodded, frowning.

"Well, this is the boy. This is the boy I was assigned to find."

In whispers, Joah told her everything, including Lupita Fertheli's suspicions that the Nocturnals had infected her son. Misla's frown deepened. When he had finished speaking, Damien began turning in circles, his wails morphing into decipherable mumbles:

"West. West. Not scary. Scary. Going back. West. Need me."

"Honey," Misla said, taking Damien's hand. The boy flinched. "You can't go west. We're supposed to be going *east*, remember? We follow the sun. That's what we do."

"Sun," Damien said. *"No. Scary. Going back. West. Need me."*

Misla continued consoling him, but Joah stared. He had never witnessed an Infected person respond to conversation by repeating a word. *Sun,* Damien had told Misla, even though that had not been part of his original, mumbling vocabulary. Come to think of it, Damien was using a wider range of words than the Infected typically portrayed.

"Listen, Misla," Joah said urgently, "Damien's got a chance at returning to his old self. A better chance than most. But we need to figure out a way to get him home, and that's going to be pretty damn difficult without any kind of steed. We need to think of ways to—"

"The river," Misla cut in. She had coaxed Damien into a sitting position on the floor, where he rocked, mumbling his words, his hand still grasped tight by Misla's. "I've been thinking about it ever since the scavengers took off. It's the only way."

"That river by the grahsm miners?" Joah asked. "But we don't have time to build boats."

"What, are you afraid of getting a little wet?" Misla smirked. "We'll find some dead logs and float, of course. The river wasn't running parallel to the High Road, it was running—"

"Southeast," Joah said, excitement mounting within him. "The Sunsetters will still be heading south, so we'd run right into them! Yes. You're brilliant, Misla. If we start now, we might be able to reach the river before the sun's gone too far down." He hoisted himself up.

"Hold up. *You* need rest." Misla glared at him. "It's still moontime. We haven't slept in ages. And *he* needs washed." She nodded at Damien, who moaned.

Joah blinked at her. "How the hell do you expect to *wash* him without the river?"

Misla nodded at the twisted tubes of steel hanging from the ceiling like oddly misplaced rain gutters. "When I first came up here, I found Damien drinking. From those. Whoever built this place must have designed something on the tower roof to store rainwater for drinking purposes, because I think the water's clean."

"Well *that* would've been nice to know."

Joah hobbled to the nearest gutter, where a square metal container, almost like a mailbox, stuck out from the base of the tube. He lifted the hatch, threw his hands inside, and lapped the frigid water from his cupped palms.

Soon Misla couldn't seem to resist. She gently disengaged herself from Damien, who continued rocking on the floor, his arms hugging his mud-caked knees to his chest. Seconds later, Joah heard her gulping water from a neighboring gutter. He wiped his mouth on his wrist.

"Okay," he whispered. "How about this? We sleep for a few arcsecs. As soon as we wake up, we fill ourselves with water and head out. We'll have to keep a brisk pace, which might be..." He glanced at Damien uncertainly. Usually, the Infected struggled and fought against eastward travel. Sometimes they had to be lugged back in handcuffs or ropes. Damien, however, seemed momentarily uninterested in continuing his westward journey toward the Eternal Night.

Maybe because the darkness is already upon us. Maybe the Nocturnals are already here.

Shaking away this thought, Joah continued in a whisper, "He isn't showing any signs of trying to escape right now, but we'll need to watch him closely. And it might be hard to get him to cooperate in riding the river east."

"We'll manage," Misla said promptly. "C'mon, help me wash him."

Together, they brought Damien handfuls of water one cupped palm at a time, lathering it over his skin. The mud trickled away, revealing scratches and sores underneath. Joah tried not to cringe. The boy would need to be seen by a healer as soon as they reached the community.

When they had washed him as best they could, Joah caught Misla's eye and gave her a slow nod. She blew out her leftover fire, encasing them in a stony blackness. Joah heard the *clunk* of the torch as she set it down, and then they moved toward one another, feeling for Damien and each other's groping fingers. When they had found him, they settled onto the floor and eased the boy into a lying position, Joah pressing against his back and Misla hugging him from the front.

They grasped each other's hands so that the boy was swaddled in a tight cocoon. Now if he had the Infected urge to escape while they were sleeping, they would know.

"Who do you think built this place?" Misla whispered. She was so close, her breath puffed onto Joah's lips. Damien mumbled incoherently between them.

"I—I don't know. Whoever they were, they must have Stayed. You can't build something *this* big between Moves." Joah stared upward unseeingly, trying to imagine living thirty years in the constant light and thirty years in the Eternal Night. Who could endure *both*?

"Could've been the Sunrisers," Misla breathed. "These walls would protect them from night beasts, and the roof would protect them from the midday sun."

"Or it could've been the Leather Skins," Joah said, grunting as he moved his legs and renewed pain exploded in his ribs. The green capsule had worn off, then. "I'm sure there's enough insulation here to shield them from the cold of sunset and night."

"Or," whispered Misla, "it could've been the Nocturnals. We like to call them monsters, you know, but monsters don't have to be primitive. They could be really, really clever."

Of course, the Nocturnals who had been infecting Joah's people *couldn't* have built this particular tower: they'd been chasing the Sunsetters around the aro for the last six decades. But there were rumors of multiple communities of Leather Skins migrating at midday, so why couldn't there be a different community of Nocturnals who had built the tower instead?

Joah remembered the glossy poster in Deckler's office that he had tried not to look at: *that* hand-drawn imagining of a Nocturnal had been hunched, with many yellow eyes and pincers for hands and hunched shoulders, an insect-like beast incapable of creation.

But what if the insectile body straightened? What if the pincers shrunk into fingers and the eyes became two and the Nocturnal on the poster simply looked like his wife had, human, with a little cracked moon plastered over the skin of its face?

Damien was snoring between them now. Joah felt himself drifting. It had been a long time since he'd laid this close to other humans, since he'd felt this kind of warmth. Misla's hand was soft and small in his. In the darkness, it could have been Blair lying next to him, the child they had never conceived sandwiched between their bodies, safe and happy and alive.

"Dream well, Misla," Joah murmured before he let himself fall into this fantastic sleep.

"Damien? Where is he? *Where is he?*"

Misla's panicked voice snapped Joah from his grogginess. Fingernails pierced his bare chest, as if checking to see whether he was man or child. When Misla shifted away from him, crawling along the floor and screaming Damien's name, Joah sat up. His skull felt fit to burst.

"He's gone," Misla cried. "I don't know —how did we—? He was here! Right *here*."

"Okay. It's okay. We'll find him. He—"

But Misla was already moving toward the staircase. Her knees clunked against the floor as she crawled in the darkness. Joah blinked rapidly, as if his brain were trying to process the impenetrable indifference between opened and closed eyes. *This.* This was like rotten death.

"Hold up," he muttered, crawling after her.

He tried to clear his spinning head. They had fallen asleep trapping Damien between them. The boy must have disengaged himself and tiptoed away without waking them. But Misla had closed that enigmatic door downstairs, and the Infected were hard-pressed to figure out things like knob-turning or door-opening. Surely, Damien was still inside the tower, wandering like a drunken Dirt Slummer on one of the levels above...

When his hands found the topmost step, however, the darkness seemed to thin. Joah blinked and squinted downward, through the gap in the floor where the staircase curled to the ground. A scabbed strip of light—perhaps not even light, but a lesser darkness—spilled from an opening near the base of the stairs.

"Oh my God," Misla said beside him. She clapped her hand to the wall and stood on shaking legs. Together they crept downstairs: Damien *had* managed to open the door, which stood ajar like a missing tooth. Outside, the world had morphed into graying shadow.

"He's gone," Joah said, dazed.

He had been imagining Lupita Fertheli's tear-shined face when she saw her son again. The furious look Aoif Deckler would give when they told him the Nocturnals were infecting children. The revival of the boy when the healers tended to him and he returned to his senses under the sun. Now he and Misla Crane would return to the community childless.

"We need to go," he muttered. He felt numb, like his fingertips had melted away. "I think it's past sunset. Negative degrees." He checked his watch blearily. It was stuck at zero.

"Yes, I agree. C'mon, can you walk?" Misla grabbed Joah's elbow and began marching him across the floor. He staggered after her, their shoes crunching over fragments of bones. "I'm sure Damien hasn't gone far. If we hurry, we might catch him before—"

"Hold up. Wait. We're not going after him. Damien's gone."

Misla stopped and stared at Joah. Her hand fell from his elbow.

"We're not going after him?" she repeated slowly.

"No." Defeat sunk to the pit of Joah's stomach. "It's too late. We need to get to the river. Damien—there's a chance he'll find his way back in a year or so. The Infected usually do."

"The Infected *adults* usually do," Misla said, and her eyes seemed to flash with the reflection of last night's fire. "Damien is a *child*. Plus, in a year's time, if all goes to plan, we'll be sailing the Green Sea. He will *die*."

"No. *We* will die, Misla." Joah watched the way her jaw jutted out and knew that their survival would depend on her cooperation. He clenched his fists, steeling himself to hold his ground. "Listen to me,

Crane. General Deckler told you to obey my every order."

"General Deckler isn't here, *Detective*," Misla hissed, and the word was a stinging reminder that Joah was no longer a retriever. "If you don't want to go after him, fine by me. But *I* wouldn't be able to live knowing I let a little boy walk into the clutches of—"

"And you're going to fight off the night beasts?" Joah said, his voice rising. "Or are you going to have a civilized conversation with the Nocturnals? Tell them to leave our children the fuck alone? Say please and thank you when they just hand Damien back to you?"

"It's none of your business how I'm going to do it." Misla's raised voice echoed throughout the rounded tower. She bent and scooped up what looked like a discarded jawbone on the ground, clutching it tight in a determined fist.

"Misla, no." Joah grabbed her wrist, but she wrenched away.

"Don't touch me, Detective Cadshaw."

And with that, Misla Crane paraded outside with her jawbone, into the graying twilight. Joah withdrew Damien's remaining strip of shirt from his pocket and hobbled after her, goosebumps erupting on his arms as the brittleness of the night air found his skin. If he had to tie Misla's wrists together and haul her back like he'd hauled so many of the Infected, he would, dammit. He'd do it for her own safety—

But the outside world hit him like an executioner's blunt ax. Even Misla, already halfway to the High Road, stopped in her tracks.

The ice moon glared with yellowed ferocity from the darkened sky, no longer a simple time-stamp for their sleep cycles, but a bowl of concentrated light partially hidden behind the clouds. Joah and Misla must have slept for more than a few arcsecs, then. They must have slept for an entire *cycle*, too stuck in the pits of their dreams to notice Damien's escape...

And the sun. The sun was gone. In the east, a faint ribbon of purple clouded the cliffs, but the light no longer extended to Misla or Joah or the tower. The High Road had been reduced to a black strip. Its surrounding shrubs, ablaze with chirping and buzzing, were mere shadows under the cloud-shielded moon.

"Misla!" Joah cried.

She had resumed her march westward, chin raised, free fist swinging at her side.

She didn't turn at her name. When the old anger flashed beneath Joah's bruised ribs, he took out the fragment of green shirt from his pocket and let it fall from his fingertips, onto the dirt.

Fine. *Fine.* If she wanted to leave him, if she was so determined to enter the darkness like Blair had, then all the wrist-tying in the world wouldn't stop her. She was not Infected. She was free to choose. She was free to ignore his warnings, his experience, his knowledge of the night.

Joah turned on his heel, cursing at the ache in his sides. He wanted to scream, rip out his hair, beg Misla to come back, but her newfound absence was already weaving a different kind of pain throughout his chest.

Trying not to think of her or Damien, he scowled at the potholes riddling the High Road.

Damn road developers, he thought. *Lazy, arrogant bastards. Well, it's their fault trailer wheels and horse hoofs got stuck in these holes during the last Move...*

Joah stopped.

No, it couldn't be. He had imagined the sound. He'd been thinking about hooves, but the scavengers had claimed all their horses were dead; there couldn't be one here.

Yet the sound of clip-clopping grew louder. And between cliffs in the distance, two blemishes appeared on the horizon, trotting westward at an easy pace. Male voices resonated across the valley, so brash that the chirping around Joah faltered as it hadn't for him.

For a moment, Joah wanted to wave his arms in the air, holler for his and Misla's saviors. Maybe the presence of other people would revive her sense. Maybe Joah could still save her.

But then he turned to squint for Misla, who was only a far-off, swaying smudge, and he remembered the scavengers swinging a fist at her. He felt their boots against his ribs and tasted the copper of blood filling his mouth. No, he should be cautious this time around.

Before the men on horseback could spot him, he dove behind a nearby shrub, swiping away a lazy horde of bugs hovering around it. He lowered himself to his exposed belly and watched between prickly branches as the men drew nearer.

There were two of them, and their booming laughter renewed the goosebumps on Joah's arms. They didn't sound frightened in the presence of the infamous Eternal Night. They sounded *casual*, as if this were merely a school picnic. As if the moon were a silly plate of cheese they might pluck from the clouds. And one of their voices rang horribly familiar in Joah's ears:

"Gotta tell you, Sid, I never cared much for the heat anyway. Wish Deckler would let us hang out in the sunset zone. So much easier on the eyes, you know."

"Sure, and then we'd be living up to our *name*," snorted the other. "Why call ourselves the Sunsetters when we're so afraid of the sun actually setting?"

"Well," said Hickory Glade, "as soon as we find Misla and kill that bastard of a bitch she's been fucking around with, we'll go back and persuade everyone that nighttime is better."

Joah didn't dare exhale. He wished the insects would come back and swarm him again as Glade and the other miner passed his hiding place, their mares nickering when they were kicked onward. Dust ballooned in their wake.

Joah pressed a palm against his mouth to stop himself from coughing on the dust. The men were still close enough that he could hear their commentary on the tower, but his ears rang with Glade's previous words: *As soon as we find Misla and kill that bastard of a bitch she's been fucking around with...* Glade was going after Misla just as he'd gone after Blair. And maybe Misla could survive the Eternal Night for a few cycles until she realized her search for the boy was futile, but she wouldn't survive an angry man with an ax if he decided to use it.

An icy resignation sagged Joah's shoulders: he wouldn't be returning to the light of day.

He would *not* let Blair's murderer take another woman he had grown to care for.

The cough escaped him, but Glade was too far past to hear him now. He and his comrade were already smudges like Misla had been, and Misla herself had dissolved into the distance. Clouds now shrouded the moon completely, and Joah could barely make out the edge of the forest he knew lay on the lip of the west.

Hurry, Misla, hurry, he urged, scrambling upward. *Lose yourself in the cotton trees before they can find you.* And then, before he could reject the thought— *I'm coming for you.*

He cast a last look at the purple remnants of sunrays in the east, then turned his back to it and started down the High Road: toward Misla, toward Damien, toward Hickory Glade and the Nocturnals and whatever else lurked out of sight. The air frosted his bare skin.

Far off, in the forest, a night beast yowled.

See Mariah Montoya's story "The Nocturnals II" online at Metaphorosis.
If you liked it, leave a comment. Authors love that!
Remember to subscribe to our e-mail updates so you'll know when new stories are posted.

Copyright

Title information

Metaphorosis June 2021

ISSN: 2573-136X (online)
ISBN: 978-1-64076-201-5 (e-book)
ISBN: 978-1-64076-202-2 (paperback)

Copyright

Publisher

Metaphorosis Magazine is an imprint of
Metaphorosis Publishing
Neskowin, OR, USA

Discounts available

Substantial discounts are available for educational institutions, including writing workshops. Discounts are also available for quantity purchases. For details, contact Metaphorosis at metaphorosis.com/about

Metaphorosis Publishing

Metaphorosis offers beautifully written science fiction and fantasy. Our imprints include:

Metaphorosis Magazine
Plant Based Press
Verdage
Vestige

You can also find us:
@MetaphorosisMag, @MetaphorosisRev,
@Metaphorosis
www.facebook.com/metaphorosis

Help keep Metaphorosis running by supporting us at
Patreon.com/metaphorosis

See more about some of our books on the following pages.

Metaphorosis
a magazine of speculative fiction

Metaphorosis is an online speculative fiction magazine dedicated to quality writing. We publish an original story every week, along with author bios, interviews, and notes on story origins.

We also publish monthly print and e-book issues, as well as yearly Best of and Complete anthologies.

Come and see us online at magazine.Metaphorosis.com

Metaphorosis: Best of 2020

The best science fiction and fantasy stories from *Metaphorosis* magazine's fifth year.

Metaphorosis 2020

All the stories from *Metaphorosis* magazine's fifth year. Fifty-two great SFF stories.

Metaphorosis: Best of 2019

The best science fiction and fantasy stories from *Metaphorosis* magazine's fourth year.

Metaphorosis 2019

All the stories from *Metaphorosis* magazine's fourth year. Fifty-two great SFF stories.

Metaphorosis:
Best of 2018

The best science
fiction and fantasy
stories from
Metaphorosis
magazine's third
year.

Metaphorosis
2018

All the stories
from *Metaphorosis*
magazine's third
year. Fifty-two
great SFF stories.

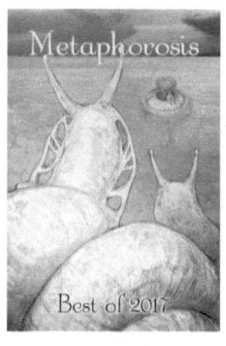

Metaphorosis:
Best of 2017

The best science
fiction and fantasy
stories from
Metaphorosis
magazine's *second*
year.

Metaphorosis
2017

All the stories
from *Metaphorosis*
magazine's second
year. Fifty-three
great SFF stories.

Metaphorosis:
Best of 2016

The best science
fiction and fantasy
stories from
Metaphorosis
magazine's first
year.

Metaphorosis
2016

Almost all the
stories from
Metaphorosis
magazine's first
year.

Plant Based Press

plant
based
press

Vegan-friendly science fiction and fantasy, including an annual anthology of the year's best SFF stories.

Best Vegan SFF of 2020

The best vegan-friendly science fiction and fantasy stories of 2020!

Best Vegan SFF of 2019

The best vegan-friendly science fiction and fantasy stories of 2019!

Best Vegan SFF of 2018

The best vegan-friendly science fiction and fantasy stories of 2018!

Best Vegan SFF of 2017

The best vegan-friendly science fiction and fantasy stories of 2017!

Best Vegan SFF of 2016

The best vegan-friendly science fiction and fantasy stories of 2016!

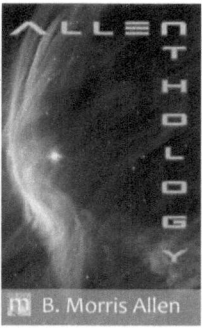

Susurrus

A darkly romantic story of magic, love, and suffering.

Allenthology: Volume I

A quarter century of SFF, including the full contents of the collections *Tocsin, Start with Stones,* and *Metaphorosis.*

Verdage

Science fiction and fantasy books for writers – full of great stories, often with an additional focus on the craft of speculative fiction writing.

Reading 5X5 x2

Duets

How do authors' voices change when they collaborate?

A round-robin of five talented science fiction and fantasy authors collaborating with each other and writing solo.

Including stories by Evan Marcroft, David Gallay, J. Tynan Burke, L'Erin Ogle, and Douglas Anstruther.

Score

an SFF symphony

What if stories were written like music? *Score* is an anthology of varied stories arranged to follow an emotional score from the heights of joy to the depths of despair – but always with a little hope shining through.

Reading 5X5

Five stories, five times

Twenty-five SFF authors, five base stories, five versions of each – see how different writers take on the same material.

Reading 5X5

Writers' Edition

Two extra stories, the story seed, and authors' notes on writing. Over 100 pages of additional material specifically aimed at writers.

Vestige

Vestige

Novelettes, novellas, and novels by Metaphorosis authors.

www.ingramcontent.com/pod-product-compliance
Lightning Source LLC
Chambersburg PA
CBHW020639110726
47899CB00002B/825